THE GIRL
WHO SPOKE TO
THE WIND

The Sheena Meyer Series

Book Two

JOA PRESS
FLORIDA

Books by L. B. Anne:

LOLO AND WINKLE SERIES

Book One: Go Viral

Book Two: Zombie Apocalypse Club

Book Three: Frenemies

Book Four: Break London

Book Five (Coming Soon): Middle School Misfit

THE SHEENA MEYER SERIES

Book One: The Girl Who Looked Beyond the Stars

Book Two: The Girl Who Spoke to the Wind

L. B. ANNE

"The breath of life is in the sunlight and the hand of life is in the wind."

– Kahlil Gibran

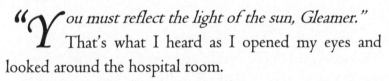

1

"*You must reflect the light of the sun, Gleamer.*"
That's what I heard as I opened my eyes and looked around the hospital room.

"*Speak to the wind...speak to the wind...speak to the wind...*" The voice echoed. Mr. Tobias's voice.

"I don't understand," I whispered. *Where am I?* I tried to sit up.

My mom gently pushed me back. "Wait, Sheena."

I looked down at the hospital bed, around the room, and at the closed curtain.

"Are you okay?" my mom asked. She looked worried and exhausted, like she had when my dad was in the hospital—the same tension in her face.

I tried to sit up again.

"Hold on, Sheena," she said. "You fainted."

"I did?" I'd never fainted before. "I'm sorry."

"Why are you sorry? You don't have to apologize. How do you feel? Do you remember why we came to the hospital?"

I thought for a moment, my eyes searching the white tiles of the ceiling. My forehead tightened as if a belt had been strapped around it. I squeezed my eyes shut. "Mr. Tobias. He's gone."

The curtain pulled back with a hard screech as someone entered. A male voice spoke to my mom, sounding especially chipper as he came around the bed where I could see him.

"Are we okay now? I hear you lost consciousness."

I looked up at the gentle expression and bright eyes of Nurse Javan. His eyes, like Mr. Tobias's, like…Ariel's… If my assumption was right…

I sat up totally alert, shocked he was there. My head wasn't ready for how fast I moved, because for a moment the room spun, and my stomach dropped like I'd been on a roller coaster "Whoa," I said as I laid back against the pillows.

"Are you okay?" asked my mom.

"Turbulence. Everyone please remain seated until the captain has shut off the fasten seatbelt sign," I mumbled.

"Take it easy," said Nurse Javan, while reaching for my shoulder. "You're funny. That's a great attitude you've got there."

What I can only describe as a cool tickle, shot through my shoulder, and my head suddenly felt clear. In fact, my whole body felt good. Like better than good.

"Do you remember me?" I asked.

"Let's see…You were here late one night, looking for someone," he replied with a warm grin.

"Yes." I was so glad he didn't mention I was talking to myself.

"I'm usually pretty good with faces."

"How are you with answers?"

"I will give you whatever information I can. Knowledge is important. It is only what you know that can save you."

"Save me from what?"

"Anything." He read over a chart and looked up at me with a grin. "Everything."

"Does that mean what you don't know can kill you?"

"Maybe." He looked into my eyes as if he wanted me to really understand what he was saying. "But I know you don't have to worry about that because you're going to study hard and learn as much as you can. You're special, I can tell," he said with a wink. "You've been given everything you need to become very successful and conquer whatever comes against you."

Given?

That's when I remembered everything that happened before I fainted. *What was the glowing thing the angel took from Mr. Tobias and gave to me? Was it something to help me?*

"Is that why I'm supposed to speak to the wind?" I asked with a brow raised. "What does that mean?"

Nurse Javan smiled. "The wind? Uh, okay."

Oh no! He has no idea what I was talking about. I thought he was— "Wait. Rewind. That didn't come out right. That was, uh, something crazy I heard someone say. Ha! Like someone would actually talk to the wind. That's crazy, right?"

I slumped back against the pillow and stared at my hands in my lap, avoiding my mom's frown. She had looked back and forth at us, confused. I'm sure she thought I might have hit my head when I collapsed and awoke talking crazy, or in riddles or something.

Nurse Javan turned to my mom. "I know Doctor Davies has already spoken to you. Since Sheena's electrocardiogram results are fine, no hospitalization is necessary."

"That means I can go?"

"You sure can. And Sheena?"

"Yes?"

"Take care of yourself." He touched his temple. "Your mind..." Then he placed his hand over his chest. "...and your heart."

"Umm, okay," I said slowly and smiled. "That's kind of deep isn't it?"

But Nurse Javan didn't return my smile.

"Yes, sir," I replied as if talking to a military commander.

A half-hour later, my mom and I stood outside the hospital emergency room entrance. Our car sat at the end of the sidewalk, but my mom didn't walk toward it.

"Sheena, I'm kind of dumbfounded right now. Maybe we've been too lax with you because of how responsible you usually are. It's like you have a whole other life going on that I know nothing about. How is that possible? You're just a child."

"I'm not a child." I knew as soon as I said it that I shouldn't have.

"Trust, now is not a good time for you to test me. And your dad…" She threw her hand up. "I don't even know how to begin to explain this to him." She looked down at her phone. "That's him now. I'm letting it go to voicemail. I'm not ready to have that conversation yet."

My mom looked off to the side for a moment and then tapped on her phone.

"What are you doing? I thought you weren't ready to tell him anything?"

"A little something is better than nothing at all. I'm texting your dad that everything is fine and that I'll explain later. Hopefully, that will pacify him for now." She placed her phone in her purse. "Now tell me what in the world all of that was about? Start with Mr. Tobias. I know you care—"

"I don't care! I don't care anymore! I mean, I care about Mr. Tobias, but I didn't ask for any of this. And I'm so confused."

"Didn't ask for any of what?"

I looked into my mom's brown eyes. *Should I tell her? Would it put her in danger? Would she think I was crazy and send me off to an asylum or something like they did with Mr. Tobias when he was young?*

"Sheena, what is it? You can talk to me. You can tell me anything." Her eyes pleaded with me.

"Mom, sit down."

We sat on the silver benches that were meant for those waiting for their rides to pick them up after being discharged from the hospital.

"What's going on?"

There was no easy way to tell her, so I just blurted it out. "Mom, I-I see things."

She had been facing me, holding my hands and looking into my eyes. But she let go of my hands and turned toward the parking lot across from the hospital.

I waited for her to ask questions, laugh, or freak out. Maybe she hadn't heard me or misunderstood, so I repeated it. "I see things."

She grabbed my hand again. "I heard you the first time. Let's go for a ride."

I didn't say anything further. I just wanted to know what she was thinking—whether she believed me or not. And why didn't she ask for details? I know my statement had major shock factor, but she showed no signs of its impact.

Neither of us spoke on the drive. I watched her, thinking I could read her expression and know what she was thinking, but I couldn't.

Maybe the angel granted me some type of mindreading power, I thought as I stared at her, pushing with my brain. Nothing happened. No superpowers. I was still just a teenager that had no idea where she fit in the scheme of the world.

Mentally exhausted, I fell asleep after a while. When I awoke, we were pulling in front of a yellow house surrounded by open fields.

Nothing ever changes here, I thought as I got out of the car and looked around.

The screened front door of the house opened. "My babies!"

My mom walked into her open arms. Then I stepped forward for her embrace, pressing the side of my face into the shoulder of her light blue house dress and inhaling the familiar gardenia scent of her favorite lotion.

"Hi, Nana."

"It's so good to see my baby. My, you look more and more like my mother, your great grandmother, every time I see you. Get on in this house. Don't you feel that chill?"

We walked in laughing after Nana saying something about it starting to get chilly enough to see chill bumps on a gnat.

But Nana didn't follow us in. She stood at the door for a minute, looking out over the field across the street before closing the door.

"Mama, is everything okay?" my mom asked Nana.

"A storm is coming," she mumbled.

I looked out the window. There wasn't a cloud in the sky.

As Nana and my mom talked in the living room, I did what I'd done for as long as I could remember, walked straight to the back of the house to the kitchen to see if—

Yes! I exclaimed in my head. There was a three-layer cake with tan frosting sitting in the center of the kitchen table, covered with a glass top.

"Sheena? Don't you touch that caramel cake!" Nana yelled.

"Omkay," is how my response sounded. My mouth was already full.

Nana and my mom walked into the kitchen laughing a few minutes later, talking about me, knowing what I would do when I saw the cake.

"Why don't we all have a slice, and I'll make tea. It seems that we have some things to discuss."

"Mom, you told her?" I whispered.

Nana put the kettle on the stove. "You focus on the wrong things, sweetie. The question is why she told me, and why she brought you here after you told her."

I looked down at my cake. I hadn't thought about that. I wondered if Nana had superhuman hearing, or if I was that bad of a whisperer.

My mom sat at my left under a wall of old copper pans Nana collected. She stood to help Nana with the tea infuser and cups.

I imagined myself as a kid running through the kitchen while Nana cooked and being scolded for it. A huge pot of mixed greens boiled on the stove and Nana stood over the counter seasoning meat. I remember being horrified because I thought she was cooking a puppy. I was ready to run away because of it and live on Sesame Street. Not the actual street, but the television show.

Coon is what she called it. *Coon?* My eyes widened in alarm realizing Nana meant raccoon. My stomach turned a flip. *Did I eat any of it? I couldn't have. I didn't like the texture of meat back then.*

Everything in the room was the same as when I was little, except for the addition of some new kitchen gadgets on the counter. I remember my mom having to intervene last year regarding Nana's shopping channel obsession.

Just as Nana and my mom began eating their cake, I finished mine.

"Now, tell Nana what you saw."

She looked at me over her glasses, and I realized I'd never been able to keep anything from her. Nana asked with that penetrating gaze of hers, and I told her whatever she wanted to know. "Yes, I drew on the walls," or "Teddy threw the frog in the swimming pool to see if it would explode."

"I don't know where to start. I feel overwhelmed," I told them.

"I'm sure. Maybe this will help."

Nana placed another slice of cake on my plate. She laughed. "It's always helped in the past to calm you down when you were upset.

"Chew slowly this time," Nana instructed.

There was some connection between chewing slowly, and the creamy frosting, I think, that soothes. I took a huge bite and talked with my mouth full. "Eyef baw some ak hospit." I added another fork full of cake to my already stuffed mouth. "Aww hink was angem."

Milk. I need milk. I grabbed my glass and drank in huge gulps. *BURP!* "Excuse me."

Nana nodded. "Slow down. Take a deep breath, sweetie."

I did as I was told.

"I think I caught a little of what you were saying. Ha! Glory be, I have no idea how."

I loved Nana's laugh. It was high-pitched and bouncy. The kind of laugh that if you heard it you could do nothing but laugh also. Just hearing it comforted me.

"I have no idea what that was," my mom said. "Let's try that again."

"She said she thinks she saw an angel at the hospital." Nana turned to me. "Is that right, sweetie?"

"I nodded."

"Tell us about Mr. Tobias," my mom instructed. I took a deep breath and told them everything. Everything except about sneaking out of the house. I mean, I'm not crazy or anything.

Nana's brows rose at hearing Mr. Tobias's name, but she didn't seem surprised by anything I said. It was like she heard this kind of stuff every day. Her taking it so calmly made it easier to talk to her. But still, I wondered why she didn't react in some way.

Instead, Nana said, "Belinda, you were supposed to pay close attention to her."

"I have been, Mama," my mom replied.

I looked back and forth between them. *Wait, what? What's going on?* It was like they knew something was going to happen to me. Like they expected it...

2

*N*ana tapped the nail of her ring finger on the table. "Sheena, you know that I used to keep you while your mom and dad were working?"

"Yes, ma'am."

"What do you remember from back then?"

"Not much. I remember this house. You used to have a cow or bull in the field. I remember it chased me."

"Ha ha! You remember old Buck! Anything else?"

"I remember people coming over a lot, visiting, and me standing in the door looking outside waiting for my mom."

"You used to stand in that door and just stare at the sky and the field and watch the trees. Do you remember playing with an invisible friend, or running and grabbing my leg, crying because of a bad something you saw?"

I shook my head, captivated, hanging on her every word.

"'Show Nana. Show Nana what you saw.' That's what I told you, but you wouldn't let go of my leg. You were terrified."

My jaw dropped. "I don't remember any of that. How-how old was I?"

"About three."

"But…"

I looked at my mom, surprised that she had something to add to the story.

"…Something happened when you were four."

"What? What happened?"

"We'd recently purchased a house and moved in. The house we're in now. You were outside in the backyard and you saw something in that tree you're always staring at."

"In our willow? Oh, the stars or something you told me about?"

"You couldn't really put to words what you saw, but we can show you."

"You can?"

My head was swimming. How were they going to show me?

Nana stood and left the room. A few minutes later, she returned with a rectangular box and placed it on the table. The lid was covered in dust. She carefully lifted it and removed several sheets of construction paper from the box.

"You've had these all this time?" I asked without looking up.

Nana didn't respond.

I took the drawings from her and spread them over the table. "I drew these at four?"

My mom nodded while biting her lip. "Yes, you did. That's when I found out about your drawing skills. What do you see?"

The colors had faded a bit, but I could still make out what I'd drawn. "Stars or lights... Umm...rainbow colors and...a figure." I studied the images. "Is that Jesus?"

"Ha! Glory be! I don't think so," Nana exclaimed.

"Why in the willow?"

"I don't know. Maybe because that's where you were at the time."

"Did you guys think I was crazy?"

"Not in this family."

"Why not?"

"It runs in our blood."

"What does?"

"Gleamers."

I know my eyes were bulging from their sockets. I couldn't believe what I was hearing. "You know about gleamers?"

"We come from a long line of gleamers. Some say it's from our Native American side. Others say it's from our African side. It's a gift, Sheena. I only have the slightest form of it. It skips generations. Nana has more..."

"More?"

"A greater ability."

Nana placed a very old photo in front of me on the table. It was damaged and stained like it had been dipped in coffee. I could just barely make out the woman in the photo. It almost looked drawn. "Is she Native American?"

"Yes."

"From our family?"

Nana nodded. "Sit down. Let me tell you a story."

I sat in front of my empty plate, pressed my finger onto a cake crumb, and placed it in my mouth. Nana sat beside me, her long braid, usually wrapped in a bun, hung over her shoulder.

"Our African American and Native American history overlaps due to an Indian woman that married a European slave owner. Their child married a freed slave." She pointed at the photo. "This woman, Eyota, had a son…"

I pronounced her name slowly in my head. *E-yo-ta.*

"This would be around the 1700's. Indians were being enslaved and exported to other countries. So Eyota's family and many others were in hiding. Her son, a young teenager, refused to be a slave, and refused to be taken away from his land. He didn't want to hide, he wanted war.

"Eyota's mother, Onawa, saw his future in a dream."

"What did she see?"

"She saw him being hunted and captured by men on horses. She saw his death."

"What did she do?"

"She tried to find him. She thought if she told him what was going to happen, he would stay in hiding with his family."

"They were going to believe her?"

"It was a different time. People believed in gleamers."

"What she saw happened, didn't it?"

"Yes. Onawa's grandson was already gone when she arrived. His mother, Eyota, risked her life traveling overnight following a riverbank south to find him. But it didn't matter what she had to say, he would be no man's slave."

"Where was he trying to run to?"

"West, to any tribe that would fight to remain free."

"Mama, I know quite a bit about our ancestors, but I've never heard this story, or seen this photo before. Why have you never told me this?" my mom asked Nana.

"This story has only been passed down to gleamers."

"What happened to him, the boy?"

"He was killed, just as his grandmother told them he would be, in the same manner in which she foretold. His grandmother swore she heard the shot ring out as it happened."

I could see the whole scene play out as if I were right there with them—Eyota's son and others running, and the sound of hooves galloping across a field.

"What happened to his mother?"

"Eyota later married the European man in that photo."

"After all of that?"

"Yes, and he owned slaves. They had two children together. This photo and story have been passed down through them. Now it is yours." She handed the photo to me. "It's one of many stories from our gleamer ancestry. So, you see, you are not alone in this. But with you, I sense there's something more."

"More? How do you know I'm something more? Mr. Tobias said that also."

"The type of encounters you've had are extremely rare. Also, you mentioned Buck chasing you. I remember that day. You ran to the house screaming. But Sheena, that wasn't Buck. Buck couldn't run."

"But he came after me. I remember it."

Nana shook her head. "No."

"Are you saying I imagined it?"

"No, I believe something chased you."

"What do you think it was?"

"I don't know, but I have an idea."

"Like?"

"Like you see things that others cannot, and only if you act on it will they know that you see them."

"Like I see dead people?"

"You know I'm not talking about dead people. This is not a movie."

"But it feels like one, some horror flick."

"This is spiritual. It's real. You haven't talked about seeing anything for years. I had a feeling something would happen when you turned thirteen. So, whatever you think you've seen, we believe you. I just wish you'd come to us sooner."

I couldn't believe it was that easy. How could I have known I could talk to them about something like this?

"Does dad know?"

"No, he doesn't believe in gleamers."

"I-I'm not a witch, am I?"

Nana laughed. "Glory be! Why would you think something like that? No, sugar. It's nothing like that. It's a gift from heaven, passed down through our family for generations, like I said. But this gift is not for you. It's so that you may help others."

"When?"

"Believe me, it will all fall into place. You won't have to ask, nor will you question it."

Nana lifted my chin and studied my face. "I can see it in your eyes."

"What can you see?"

"The gleam. What is it you're worried about?"

"How do you know I'm worried?"

"I discern it," she replied with a wink.

"Mr. Tobias told me that I put the people I care about in danger if I tell them anything."

"Danger how?"

"He said the Murk will cause me pain so I cannot use my gift, by attacking those I care about."

"The Murk?" my mom asked, looking at Nana.

Nana shrugged, but her countenance changed from one of curiosity to one of concern.

"Nana, what's wrong? Was he right?"

"Nothing, dear. I'm thinking about what you said. Oh, not about the danger part. We're protected. Don't worry about that. I agree with Mr. Tobias. You're something more than a Type-one gleamer."

"But, what?"

"I don't know, but we'll find out soon enough."

I hugged Nana as long as I could and as tight as I could before we left. I don't know where other people thought the safest place in the world was, but for me it was right there with Nana.

She waved at us from the front door. "Sheena..."

I stepped up on the running board of my mom's car and looked over the top at Nana.

"May your vision be true."

I froze in place, hearing the very same words that had come from Mr. Tobias.

3

" *A*re you going to tell Dad?"
My mom shook her head. "Not yet. He doesn't even believe in the sight, prophets or anything of the sort. How can I tell him that his daughter is a gleamer?"

A gleamer. I'm a gleamer. My mom really just said that. And after the story Nana told me, I guess I believe it now, too. Pastor Evans did say more than one person would confirm what I wanted to know. Wow, I'm really a gleamer?

I tried to feel out every inch of my body from the inside, if that were possible, to see if I felt any different. All I felt was gas that I was determined to hold in until I got out of the car. *Please don't make me laugh,* I thought, *or else.*

"What do we do now?" I asked my mom.

"We figure out a way to exist with it, and you start documenting everything. Write it all down—everything that happens."

"But what about—"

"Sheena, no more questions for now. I need to think for a minute—to process all of this. When we get home, just go to your room. I'll deal with your dad. It'll be okay."

I collapsed over my bed and turned over onto my back, looking up at the ceiling. At that moment, I felt normal. It was just a normal day—a thirteen-year-old girl in her room reaching for her pink fluffy pillow and hugging it to her chest before starting her homework.

I sat up, hearing my parents' voices. My door was cracked open, so I tiptoed over to it.

They were discussing me, loudly, but at least they weren't arguing. "She needs to rest," my mom was saying.

I walked over to my desk and sat down. If my dad decided to charge down the hall—who was I kidding, he wasn't healed enough to charge anywhere yet—at least I would have started my homework. *That's one less thing for him to fuss about.*

I looked up, seeing Dingy across the way frantically waving his arms at me. I put my hand up as to say hi. I could never understand why he cared for my attention so much. That seemed to be enough for him. He put his hand up also, placed his palm on the window, stared at me for a moment, and disappeared.

He's a fast little bugger.

Bugger. I'd gotten that word from Mr. Tobias. It made me smile and then tear up a little. I didn't get to say goodbye to him. He said we were the last. With him gone, I was the last. I think he meant the last of the Type-one gleamers, because my Nana was a gleamer and she still lived.

I thought about the angel and how it gave me something. It was like he passed it on from Mr. Tobias to me. It sparkled like the spark in Mr. Tobias's eyes. I wondered if my eyes now looked like they'd been charged up with high powered batteries too. Or maybe I couldn't see it, but another gleamer could. That's what Nana saw.

I pushed my schoolbooks aside. Now was as good a time as any to document, as my mom said, everything that happened. It didn't take long to get it all down, but I didn't stop there. I wrote the whole story Nana told me about Onawa and her grandson, and then I wrote about my friends:

Chana wasn't around as much lately, and I wasn't sure if it was my fault or hers. I still couldn't get Teddy to tell me where he'd been when he missed those days of school. Ariel shows up at the craziest times. I won't see her and then she will just be there, looking for me with that smile like I'm the most wonderful person in the world. It kind of made me want to live up to what she thinks.

The next day, I didn't want to talk about any of it, and was relieved when my mom suggested that I get away from anything gleamer related, if it were possible.

I wished I could push the side of my head, hitting a delete or backspace key, making it all go away for a while. Wouldn't that be cool, though? Anyway, I agreed. A break from my own mind, if only for hours, was worth a try.

I reluctantly answered my phone when Teddy called.

"I figured you wouldn't be in school today after I heard about Mr. Tobias. I'm sorry."

"Not today."

"What do you mean not today? I can't be sorry today?"

"I mean, I'm not talking about any of it today. I can't."

"I understand. Are you going to the funeral?"

"My mom won't let me."

"That's probably a good idea."

"Why do you say that?"

"Oh yeah, I forgot you're not talking about it today. Hey, Ariel looked for you at school today."

Is he trying to change the subject? "She's back?"

"Yep."

"I'll call her. Did I miss anything at school?"

"Nah, everything was the same as usual. Oh yeah, a couple kids are missing."

"Who?"

"You know, the twins? Chuck and Charmayne."

"Really?"

"Yeah, no one knows the details, but the police came to the school."

"I hope they're okay. Maybe they ran away."

"I don't know, maybe."

"Hey, do you want to meet up at the mall in an hour with me and Chana?"

"What do I look like, hanging out with you at the mall while you watch boys."

"That is not what we'll be doing. You hang out with us all the time."

"Yes, but not at the mall."

"Just come. My mom wants me to get out and do something fun. She wants me to try and just be a normal teen today."

"Okay, okay. But since when are you normal? Wait, are you saying your mom knows you're a gleamer?"

"I told her yesterday."

"Whoa, how did she take it?"

"We can talk about that later. Come with us."

"Okay, let me ask my dad. He may have plans for me to rake the leaves for the three-hundredth time."

"Who are you asking to the Sadie Hawkins dance?" asked Chana as we sat at the center court, looking through the windows of the bookstore and Hot Topic.

"Absolutely no one."

She angled her head toward Teddy. "Really?"

"Stop it."

"Theodore, has anyone asked you to the Sadie Hawkins dance yet?"

I sat between Chana and Teddy, turned, with my back to Teddy, and mouthed for Chana to stop.

"Yeah, but I haven't accepted anyone's invite."

"Why not?"

"Because then it will look like we're together or something. I don't want to give the wrong impression."

"It's just a dance."

"Yeah, but those memories last forever."

That was a good answer. Good for him. He knew what those memories could mean to a girl. *I've taught him well.*

"Okay, look, we can go to the arcade, or bowling, or see a movie. But this dude is not about to go clothes shopping with you so you can be like, 'For real, girl? Is this cute on me?'"

I almost fell over into the fountain laughing at him talking like a girl.

"Then you'll run around filming TikTok videos and scouting around for VSCO girls…" He shook his head. "Count me out."

"We don't do that," said Chana.

"Yes, you do. Hey, do you guys smell that? I need a snack."

"You're always hungry."

"That's because I'm still growing."

"Lucky you," I replied.

The smell of potatoes frying wafted toward us, as if summoning us and pulling us toward it like magnets. We turned the corner past jewelry stores and a mattress store.

As Teddy walked, he called out everything we should order and share so we would have a full selection spread over our table. "Fries, pizza, orange chicken...Is the Greek place still open? That sounds good too."

We were almost to the food court when I came to an abrupt stop, causing Chana to walk into me.

"Sheena, what's wrong?" asked Chana.

I wanted to scream out, but I couldn't speak.

Teddy walked back and stood directly in front of me, blocking my view. "Sheena, look at me. Look in my eyes!"

I did as he instructed. His pupils were large, surrounded by a blend of light brown with green specks.

"If you don't acknowledge you see anything, they won't know that you do," Teddy whispered.

My eyes widened. Could Teddy see it too?

I forced myself to speak. "We're in the wrong place," I whispered. I don't even know why I said it, like the words came from me, but from someplace deeper.

Chana looked back and forth between us. She caught on quickly. "The wrong place." It was a statement and not a question. "We are going to laugh like something is really funny. Follow my lead."

Teddy pointed to the right of where I had been looking and made a stupid joke. We all laughed, and Chana placed her arm inside of mine and pulled me, getting my legs moving again. We walked off to the nearest costume jewelry store with Teddy fussing behind us about him not going inside a girly store.

After getting our fill of unicorn jewelry, tutus, sunglasses, cheap makeup and nail polish, we left that store and walked as far away from the food court as possible, still talking like nothing ever happened.

BOOM!

We all fell toward the wall to the right of us. Alarms went off and a cloud of smoke shot out toward us. Screaming seemed to come from everywhere at once. We helped each other up, careful not to get knocked back down by the horde running at us, and ran for the nearest exit with the rest of the stampede. We were like horses breaking through doors of a stable that was on fire.

The whole crowd raced across the parking lot, Teddy, Chana, and I didn't stop running until we were about a block from the mall.

"I need to call my mom," I said as I caught my breath. "She's going to freak out if she sees this on the news."

"Will they put this on one of those alerts on your phone like the amber alert?" asked Teddy.

"I don't know. I need to call mine too. She's down the street at kickboxing class," said Chana.

"Sheena, when you said we were in the wrong place, did you know the place was going to explode? Are we good?" asked Teddy.

"I think we're safe now. I don't know how I knew."

"What do you mean, you don't know how you knew? I know how you knew!"

"So do I," Chana added. "Do you see anything now?"

"Was it something scary?" asked Teddy.

"A swirling dark, shadowy, mist near the pizza restaurant."

We turned, hearing sirens. Ambulances and firetrucks arrived.

"It did this?"

"I don't know."

"Do you guys realize this could have happened any time of day, but it happened while you were there, precisely when you would've been sitting there eating or at the counter placing an order?"

"What are you trying to say, Theodore?" asked Chana.

"I thought that was pretty clear." He turned to me. "Was that not clear? Chana's always trying to—"

"Teddy, how did you know what I was seeing or what I should do?"

"Those days I wasn't at school, I skipped. Did you see Mr. Tobias whisper something to me before we left the hospital that night?"

"Yeah."

"He needed to meet with me alone. He said you were going to need a friend."

"I'm her friend," said Chana. "I knew I should have tried harder to sneak out. It's not so easy when your dad is a police officer."

"It's not easy, period, Chana. Mr. Tobias wanted to make sure Sheena has a friend that knows what to do." Teddy turned to me. "I went to him to find out if you were in any real danger as a gleamer."

"Why would you do that?"

"Why do you think? Because we're friends, and I care. Wouldn't you do the same for me?"

I guess so, I thought. *I know I would for Chana.* I nodded in response.

"What else did he tell you?" asked Chana.

"I can't tell anyone."

"But I'm her friend too, and I need to know so I can help."

Teddy shook his head.

"Oh, you're going to tell me, Theodore." Chana's voice was low and threatening.

"Look, I'm just doing what he said. And now that he's not here, I'm sticking to it—at least until her guardian reveals himself."

"Her guardian?"

"My guardian?" Chana and I spoke at the same time."

"Yeah, you have a guardian angel."

Chana and her mom.

4

C hana's mom left kickboxing class and picked us up in a panic. Not that there wasn't a need for panic—I mean her daughter could've been crushed by a ceiling or injured by projectiles or something.

She screamed at the top of her lungs through the roadblock and tried to force her way through.

"Why is she screaming my name like that?" asked Chana.

"What did you say on the text?"

"I told her the mall blew up."

"Sheesh, really?"

That explained why her mom looked hysterical.

It turned out the explosion took place in the kitchen of one of the restaurants. People were injured. We listened to the reports over the radio all the way home.

Chana, Teddy, and I texted back and forth throughout the night about what happened. I was bummed that Teddy didn't have any more information about the guardian angel thing. I had so many questions: How would he show himself? Would it just appear next to me and scare the living daylights out of me? Would it wait until I was in trouble, about to fall off a building or something, and cause me to safely coast to the ground?

I was sure my mom would want to know what I saw at the mall, but I didn't tell her. We sat watching the news, me with my head on my dad's shoulder playing a game on my phone, my mom on the other side of my dad eyeing me. I tried to look innocent, like I wasn't keeping anything from her. I don't think she fell for it.

My mom peeked her head into my room later that night and almost screamed. "What is that?" she asked of the thin, almost translucent, sheet mask covering my face, only revealing my eyes, nostrils and lips.

"A Korean snail mask. It has snail mucus in it," I said for effect, just wanting to see the shock on her face. And she didn't disappoint.

"Eww...You're thirteen. Why do you need that?"

"Wrinkles."

My mom shook her head. "Wrinkles?"

"I bought it at the mall today. I'm making sure my skin stays well hydrated."

"You don't have wrinkles, and you don't need that. That's for someone my age."

I held the package up. "I have more."

"No thank you," she replied, as if disgusted by the thought. "I know I said to take some time off from thinking about gleamers, but did you document everything?"

"Yes."

"Okay, that's it. Although I'm mom-hardwired to ask more questions about today, I'm not going to do it. Uh... Toss me one of those masks," she said with a smirk. "Don't be alarmed if you hear your dad scream," she said as she closed the door.

She'd be back. She'd started checking on me in the middle of the night to make sure I was okay, and I was glad for it. I kept having that same dream about the black sludge, waking up in a cold sweat and in a panic.

<hr />

I started the next day oddly refreshed. I guess I was a little excited about having a guardian angel. That meant he could be right with me at that moment, but not saying anything. But then I was like, *He's seeing me naked?* I backed into my closet in my robe and got dressed in the dark.

My mom dropped me off at the corner from the school so she wouldn't have to get in the drop-off line of cars. I sat there a minute, looking down the street at Mr. Tobias's house.

"Are you okay?"

I opened the car door and hopped out like I was just fine. Then I jumped back in with my knees on the seat and leaned in and kissed her. "See you later."

"Have a super wonderful day…"

It seemed like she was going to say something more, but she didn't.

"I sure will," I said as I closed the car door.

I faced the school. "It's going to be a great day. That's the attitude I'm going to have from now on." In that moment, I felt I'd accomplished something major within myself and walked into the building with a smile.

But something was off. I stopped in front of the locker of one of the missing kids. It was covered in paper flowers, stickers, photos and notes. I pulled a sticky note from my backpack. *What do you write on a note to a kid that's missing? I hope they find you? No, I have to think of something better than that.* Instead I wrote, *I'm praying for you.* I stuck the note on the locker and looked around at a group that snickered and looked at me like I was more odd than usual.

In homeroom, every time I looked up, eyes were on me. A couple of boys looked over their shoulders and giggled. *What is your problem?* I thought as I sat down at my desk and stared back at Bradly. *So this is what we're doing? We're having a stare-down?*

In my next class there were whispers. In choir class, just before we were to begin our own special rendition of "Send in the Clowns," a few kids grouped together behind me and sang, "Ah..." as if they were a host of angels. The other kids laughed.

It was in lunch period that everything hit the fan. A better way to put it is my worst fear and nightmare was sucked in toward a fan and then shot out and slammed into my face at five-hundred miles an hour.

I sat down at a lunch table that a couple of kids left when they saw me, opened my bag, and pulled out a sandwich. As I bit into it, I looked around. Heads turned toward me and smirked.

What the heck is going on? I thought as I looked around for Ariel and Chana. Neither of the girls had entered the cafeteria yet. I hadn't even seen Teddy.

As I ate, I noticed no one joined my table, like I was a leper or an outcast or something. Teddy startled me at the trash bins as I threw my bag away with the extra sandwich in it that I would normally give away.

"Teddy, where have you been? Do you see the way everyone is watching me? What the heck is wrong with everybody?"

"Let's go outside. I need to talk to you."

"No, I don't want to go outside. I want you to tell me what's going on."

"Sheena!"

I spun around. What did *he* want?

"Stop it, Cameron," said Teddy. "You've done enough already." He stood between us with his arm outstretched like he was going to hold him back.

"I don't understand. What has he done?"

"Just go on outside," Teddy said, keeping eye contact with Cameron. His expression was threatening.

"No, let him talk."

"It seems that Theodore here thinks you see angels and demons."

I ignored Cameron and placed my focus on Teddy. Had he been pretending to be my friend when he was really making fun of me all this time behind my back? Was his concern all just an act?

A kid jumped off a lunch table with his arms outstretched. "Sheena, I'm an angel, a dark one. Can you see me?" Another kid ran at me, bumping into the back of me with his jacket over his head. I guess he was supposed to be a ghost or something. A few more kids joined in, doing the same. Teddy pushed them away.

The room spun for a moment as laughter came from all over the cafeteria.

"Why is he saying that, Teddy? Why is this happening?"

"Tell your boo-thang what you wrote in your diary."

"She's not my boo-thang, and I don't have a diary. It's a journal."

"Same thing."

"No, it's not." Teddy turned toward some kid. "Why are you filming? You're not even supposed to have your phone out."

I didn't turn away from Teddy. "Just tell me what's in it, and how *he* knows about it," I said, pointing at Cameron without turning to him.

"Uh...umm...It's to help you," he whispered.

"What's in it, Teddy?"

"Just everything you've been through since it all began."

"And you're showing it to people?"

"He stole it and read it."

My heart beat hard and fast in my chest. "This is why everyone is whispering about me?"

"Sheena, I'm sorry."

"Where is this journal?"

Teddy turned to Cameron.

Cameron shrugged just as Chana walked up behind him and pulled the journal from the back of his pants.

Cameron whipped around, but not quick enough to stop Chana. "The gang's all here. The Three Muskefreaks,"

Chana stepped into his face. "You know Cameron, you've been itching for a little slap therapy for a while now..."

"Who's going to give it to me?"

My head hung low, I mean really low—anything so I wouldn't have to look over at my dad and see the disappointment on his face. This *would* be the thing that caused him to come out of the house for the first time after his accident other than for doctor or therapy appointments.

Principal Vernon sat, looking smug with his hands clasped together on top of his desk. "It's all over the school that your daughter supposedly sees angels. I know, I know," he said, lifting his hands. "Kids tease, tell secrets, lie—that's not my concern. I don't care if she sees vampires or flying horses. She cannot attack students for doing what kids do. This is a normal part of adolescence. Your peers are going to tease and taunt and spread rumors. Do you know what to do when that happens?"

I wanted to say, "Kick them in the throat?" but I didn't. Principal Vernon was staring at me now, waiting for a response. The worst thing I could do was avoid eye contact. It made me look guilty. I kept trying to defend myself, but Principal Vernon wasn't having it.

My eyes met his, and I jumped. His pupils flickered. I watched him and moved my head with his, trying to get him to look me in the eye again.

"Ignore them?" I slowly replied.

"That's right. You should've just walked away, and come to me, your counselor, or one of your teachers. This is not like you, Sheena. You're usually in my office for one of your never-ending debates with your teachers. I'm used to you challenging them, but nothing like this."

I no longer heard any of the foolishness he'd been saying. I mean, I considered it foolishness because I didn't feel I was wrong for my actions. Okay, I know I shouldn't have put my hands on Cameron. There, I said it. But he deserved it.

After a few more minutes of lecturing and his anti-bullying speech, my parents stood and shook Principal Vernon's hand. My dad grabbed his crutch and shuffled out of the office ahead of us without another word.

I don't know why I put my hand out for Principal Vernon to shake it also. I had never done that before. He looked at me oddly and grasped my hand with a firm, callused grip. When he loosened his grip to release my hand, I didn't let go.

"Look after your wife. You know, your regular Saturday meeting? Don't do it. Not this weekend. End it."

Principal Vernon looked pale. His mouth dropped open, and his eyes were wide with shock. "How did you—" He cleared his throat and looked at my mom. "I, uh…"

I released his hand. "You said detention Monday? I'll be there." Before anything else could be said, I turned to leave the office.

I recognized the pink Chucks with rhinestone C's added to the sides and the bright blue striped nails of the person that sat in the waiting area with her hands covering her face, crying. Down from her sat all the kids that pulled out their phones and filmed the incident.

To the left, through an office window, Cameron sat with a bruise on his right jaw.

I grasped my throbbing hand.

Cameron's smug expression changed to that of a huge grin of an evil villain when he saw me. He waved and blew a kiss.

The nerve of him. I can't believe I used to be his friend.

Chana began to wail as if someone had just killed her mom. I kicked her foot as I passed her to let her know it was me passing, and to tell her she was doing too much. Her fingers parted and an eye looked out at me as she quieted down some and wiggled her thumb at me.

5

*M*y dad sat in the passenger seat of the car, in silence, fuming all the way home. Although I was sitting behind him, I could see how tense his body was. He was like a container building up pressure under a lid, and I wanted to get as far away from him as possible.

As soon as we walked into the house, that lid blew off and he exploded.

"Dad, I'm sorry!"

"Sorry, Sheena? What the heck has gotten into you lately?"

"You're the one who taught me to defend myself."

"Yes, to defend *you*. You were defending Chana."

"He punched her. Would you let someone punch your best friend, and your best friend is a female?"

"You double-teamed him."

And? That was my expression, but I didn't dare say it.

"Chana, Chana, Chana. That's all you think about. Your friendship with her is becoming a problem."

"No, it's not!"

"Why is your friendship with her such a big deal?"

"It's a million things that you wouldn't even understand."

The day was going from bad to worse. If my dad made me stop being friends with Chana, I was going to die. I could feel it. My heart was going to explode in my chest, and I was going to collapse right there in front of him.

"Sheena, go to your room," my mom stated in a way that was meant to calm both of us down. I knew it to mean 'let me talk to your dad.'

"You have the nerve to look at me with attitude?" said my dad. "You better straighten your face before I come over there. And I don't want to hear a peep out of you. If I so much as hear you breathe—"

"Okay. That's enough," my mom interjected. "Go to your neutral corners."

"You're grounded, young lady!" my dad exclaimed, pointing at me with his crutch.

"Young lady? I thought I was your baby girl!" I stomped away and slammed my bedroom door.

"Did she just slam my door?" I heard my dad yell. "Do it again!"

My mom came to my room thirty minutes later. She sat on the bed next to me and removed the headphones from my ears.

"How did I do?" I asked.

"That was good. I think he fell for it. I told you an argument always changes his focus. It totally took his mind off you seeing angels."

"What did you say?"

"I told him you were just as stubborn as him and that I would have a talk with you.

"Unfortunately, I'll have to take those headphones and your tablet. You can keep your phone, but don't use it unless it's an emergency. And don't mention Chana's name for a while."

"But mom..."

"Hey, this is taking it easy on you. You should count your blessings your dad didn't come in here."

I handed the headphones over to her. "Did he believe that I see things?"

"Of course not. What parent would?"

"You."

"I meant what normal parent. But what I want to know is what happened with the Mr. Vernon."

I forgot she was in the doorway waiting for me and saw the whole thing. "I saw something behind his eyes. Then, when he shook my hand, it was like watching a door open and seeing what was taking place behind it."

"A gleam."

"I guess so."

"You saw him cheating on his wife?"

I nodded. Every Saturday, he meets a woman for lunch. That's what I saw."

"But this Saturday..."

"His wife is very sick, but he doesn't know it."

"Wow. Could you shake the lottery drawer's hand or something?"

"Mom, it doesn't work like that. It doesn't happen with everyone—"

"What's wrong?"

"The man in the truck..."

"At school?"

"No, down the street from here. The same one that stopped Ariel. I saw something with his eyes too, but it was worse, they flashed red."

When my mom left the room, I fell into a deep sleep. My room was dark when I awoke. I lay there thinking about everything that happened that day.

I was now the laughingstock of the whole school, but I don't think anyone would dare say anything about it to my face. Not after the way I socked Cameron in the jaw and attempted to make sure he took a permanent vow of purity.

I flipped over, hearing voices. From my window I saw lights flash. Then I heard a car door close. What was I supposed to do, stay in my room? Of course not. I tiptoed down the hall, squatted on the stairs, and looked through the rail.

Is that Nana? She hardly left her home for anything other than groceries.

"This is about Sheena..."

They're talking about me?

"How bad can it be?" my mom asked.

"She's in danger."

6

"*M*ama, are you sure it's Sheena? Once, you thought it was Jonas, but it turned out to be his brother. And what about these kids disappearing all over the area? Have you seen any of that? And you didn't see Jonas's accident at all, so—"

"I wasn't supposed to see his accident. Sheena needed to see what she saw at the hospital," Nana replied.

Her voice came from further away. I had to listen harder. I leaned too far over the steps and almost tumbled down head-first.

"You could be right," said Nana. "It could very well be someone close to her."

Our doorbell rang, followed by banging on the front door.

What did I do now? was all I could think. I mean, I had to be the reason why. No one ever came banging on our door. I heard the floor creak in my mom's room and ran back to my room. That meant my dad was up. I looked out my window. There was a police car in the driveway.

Back and forth I paced in front of my bed. *Did Cameron's parents call the police? Maybe I should've apologized.*

I threw on my robe, and after my dad hopped down the stairs, I ran down the hall and waited there, listening.

"Sheena, come down here," my dad said. He must have heard me.

"I didn't do it."

"That's not it," said my mom.

"Dingy is missing. When's the last time you saw him?" asked my dad.

"He's gone?"

"We're just finding out that he's been gone for four days."

"Four days? But I saw him..." I counted in my head. "...three days ago."

"Where?" asked the police officer.

"In his window, waving at me. He smiled, but he looked sad..." my voice trailed off.

"That's impossible."

7

*H*ow was it impossible that I saw Dingy? *I know I'm not going crazy. I know what I saw.* He frantically waved at me from his window.

"She's mistaken, Officer. I think she meant five days ago. Isn't that right Sheena?" asked my mom. Her eyes narrowed. She wanted me to agree.

I nodded.

"So, you haven't seen him since then?"

"No, sir." I stood with Nana's arm around my waist. She guided me back and into the next room.

When Nana faced me, tears began to well up in my eyes. She grabbed my face with both hands. "No, sugar. Save those tears. Now is not the time to let your emotions get the best of you." She lowered her voice. "Emotions block the gleam. We've had the same premonition, only mine came in the form of a dream. You *saw* him. That's one of the ways we're different."

My dad approached us. "Sheena, are you okay?"

"Yes," I replied while choking back tears.

"Mama Val, I didn't even know you were here until I came downstairs. What got you out of the house?" He sat at one of the stools at the kitchen counter.

"I—"

"Don't tell me...You had one of your feelings, didn't you? I don't believe in that mumbo jumbo, but this time you may have really felt something."

Nana smiled and tightened her arm around my waist.

"Sheena, your mom went up to get the guest room ready for Nana. We don't want her going home at this time of night."

"No, Jonas, I think I'll room with Sheena."

Dad's brow's rose. "Are you sure?"

"Yes. She's worried. I don't want to leave her alone. She still has a trundle bed, right? I'll be fine with Sheena."

"Okay, whatever you want, Ma."

As we walked past my dad to go up to my room, he grabbed me with one arm, hugged me to him, and kissed my forehead. It turned me to mush. I was his baby girl again.

"They'll find him. Don't worry," he said, and squeezed me in a bear hug one more time for good measure.

I followed Nana up the stairs, making sure she watched her step. Our stairs were steep. It was a miracle my dad could get up and down them. That's why he mostly stayed upstairs.

"Welcome to my boudoir, Nana," I said as I pushed the door open and stood back for Nana to enter.

She walked in and looked around the room but didn't say a word. She watched me as I sat on the end of the bed.

"You can take the bed," I said, looking away.

Nana sat next to me. I refused to turn toward her. It didn't matter. She touched my back and tears poured from my eyes like a faucet.

"Okay," she said, rubbing my back. "It's going to be okay."

I turned to Nana and cried into her shoulder. She didn't try to stop me this time. I guess sometimes it's okay for a gleamer to cry.

For some odd reason, I thought Nana and I would stay up most of the night talking, like I usually did with Chana. Nana lay on my bed and I lay below her on the trundle.

"Nana, do you have any more stories about Eyota?"

Nana spoke while yawning, "Yes, but let me tell you about it later, sugar."

She became very quiet. After a few minutes, I raised up on my elbow and stretched my neck to see her over the mattress. She'd fallen asleep with a black book open in front of her.

I got on my knees and climbed up onto the bed. I've seen Nana fall asleep reading her Bible for as long as I can remember, so that wasn't a surprise. I leaned in next to her. She breathed heavily and made a sound just short of a snore. I almost laughed as I reached for the Bible to close it and put it at her side.

I froze there, staring at the book. The black book wasn't a Bible at all, but some kind of journal. I read over the first few lines, lifted the page, and slid the book from her fingers.

I sat next to Nana, then glanced over at her and back down at the book as I flipped to the front of the book. It was a book of dreams and prayers. Whatever Nana dreamed each night, she wrote in this book. There were notes along the sides and tops of the pages in different colored inks. I looked up, wondering how many of these journals she had. If she had been doing this for years, there could be a closet full of them.

But this book seemed older. Some of the pages were frayed, and the writing faded. I flipped to the back. All the pages were written on. I checked the dates. The book was from when I was little. *Why would she be reading something from back then?*

I thumbed through the pages. Something caught my eye. I threw my legs over the side of the bed and stepped down onto the trundle, then onto the floor. The bed squeaked and I looked over at Nana. For a second, I thought she was watching me but then I heard her snore.

I sat down under my nightlight and read.

The future of gleamers in the form of a vision.

I closed the book. *Wait, I'm snooping. I could get in trouble for this.* I set the book down, but my hands wouldn't listen to my brain, and I picked it back up. I opened the book and found the page I'd begun reading.

On the Day of Atonement, glory will fall. Select will be shown. One will see. The last of this generation.

That's like a prophecy, I thought. My name was written on the side with a question mark in red ink, but I struggled to read the scribbled and half-fading writing below it. *Me? Is it saying that's me—the last of this generation? Mr. Tobias did say we were the last. Now with him gone…*

I read well into the night and placed the journal beside Nana. My mind was all over the place after having read Nana's dreams or visions. There were prayers, notes, and scriptures all over the pages in different colored inks, and check marks and dates, I guess for when she found the events took place. Some even had names next to them.

When I finally fell asleep, it was only for a couple hours. I sat up, trying to talk myself out of reading more of the journal. I turned to Nana to see if the journal was still at her side.

She was gone.

I jumped up and searched throughout the house but couldn't find her. *Did she go home already?*

On my way back up to my room, I passed the window over the stairs and backed up. There was someone outside. I pressed my face against the glass, trying to see who it was, thinking the man in the truck had found me. But it wasn't him, it was Nana with the throw blanket from my bed wrapped around her and draped over her head.

Nana walked slowly down the side of the house and around to the front. I ran to the window at the front of the house and watched her. Even though she was walking, she seemed so still, like a statue. Now she turned down the other side of the house. I ran to the backdoor, slipped on my mom's Crocs, and walked up to her as she approached the backyard.

"Nana, what are you doing out here?"

"Praying."

"Praying? You can pray in the house. Why are you outside?"

"You can either join me or go back inside. You're interrupting."

"I don't think that was an answer. Okay, I'm going back to bed."

"Sheena..."

"Just joking, Nana."

"Get in here," she said while lifting the throw blanket and placing it around me also.

I snuggled in next to her, her arm around my shoulder as we walked.

"So, really, what are you doing out here, marching around the house like it's the walls of Jericho or something?"

"I'm impressed you know that story. It's nothing like that. I'm putting a hedge of protection around your home. I'm speaking to the wind."

Speaking to the wind? Speak to the wind. That's what I heard in Mr. Tobias's voice after I fainted.

"Wind is like the breath of the universe. Prayer is like a portal. It's powerful, and with that, you can speak to the four winds," she said, looking up at the sky. I looked up also and wanted to ask if she could make out the big dipper, but I realized that wasn't the time.

Speaking to the wind didn't make any sense to me, but I didn't mind hearing about it because it reminded me of the story of Onawa. Listening to Nana was like hearing Onawa or Eyota back in the day.

Nana prayed as we came around the front of the house for the third time. "It is done," she said with a heavy sigh.

At dawn, Nana awoke and found me staring out the window at the back of Dingy's house. "You're becoming what you were destined to become. May your vision be true."

I looked back at her, blinked, and she was gone. Then I really awoke. It had been a dream. It was much later than dawn, and Nana was really gone, having left to go home already.

My vision...My vision *was* true. That dream I had with the sludge was about Dingy. It was about saving him.

I instantly knew what I had to do as I looked out the window at grey clouds blowing in. Although they didn't look like clouds at all but thick billowing smoke. The wind picked up, blowing tree branches and leaves across the lawn. *It's too early to be this dark.*

"Sheena?" my mom called. "Get dressed. Your dad wants you to help him wash the car."

"In this weather?"

"Stop playing, girl. It couldn't be a nicer day. There's no getting out of it."

I looked out the window again. "What is she talking about?"

My cell phone dinged.

I read the text message. "A storm is brewing, be careful." *Yeah, a storm only I can see.* The text came from Ariel. That was a really weird text to receive. I mean, it was true, but kids don't text that kind of stuff. It was like she could see what I could see, or what I was going to do.

That's it, I thought. *Ariel is my guardian angel. She has to be. That would explain a lot.* Wait, Teddy didn't say anything about my guardian being human and going to school with me. Do they do that?

Any further thoughts about Ariel would have to wait. Besides, if she really was my guardian angel, she would show up and help me, right?

Washing the car with my dad gave me time to think, and fully work out a plan. It wouldn't be easy, but it could work. Hey, I was a future police detective, right? That meant I had a knack for figuring things out. *Mind, don't fail me today*, I thought as I ran up the stairs to change into dry clothes. My dad had fully enjoyed my screams as he sprayed me with the hose, supposedly by accident, every chance he got.

When I got to the top of the stairs, our doorbell rang. My dad was down in the family room, so I went into my parent's bedroom and looked out of the window and down at the front of the house.

A boy talked to my mom from the sidewalk, which was weird. Why wouldn't he go up to the porch?

He looked up at the window as if he could see me. Two girls stood behind him. They were all tall and looked enough alike to be triplets. Lean with smooth ebony skin and high cheekbones, I thought the girls looked like models.

"My name's Drake. My sisters go to school with Sheena. They asked me to bring them by to check on her."

I looked toward the driveway. There wasn't a car out there, so how did he bring them?

"May we speak with her? Everybody's pretty worried about her."

"Yeah sure, come in."

"No, that's okay. We can wait here."

"Sheena?" my mom called.

"Coming..." I responded, but I didn't move. I stared down at the kids. I didn't recognize them at all. Why were they asking for me?

"Drake, do you have classes with Sheena?"

"No, my sisters do. I'm eighteen."

"Let me see what's keeping her. Hold on a sec."

My mom backed up into the house, bumping into me as I walked toward the door.

"Mom, who's that?"

"Kids from school. They were worried about you. And don't act like you weren't listening from upstairs."

"Who, me?"

"Yeah, uh-huh. You could have at least changed. You're going to get sick going out there wet like that."

"There was no time, Mom."

I opened the door and watched the three teens as I stepped across the porch and down the stairs. Their backs were to me. As I reached the second to the last step, they turned around. I didn't step any closer. There was something eerily dark about the boy—about all three of them, really.

He spoke softly. "Hello, gleamer."

Something sunk in my chest, weighing me down and taking my breath away.

"Why did you just call me that?"

"Do you see us?"

"Yes?"

"No, do you *see* us?

I gasped, seeing his eyes flash. "Who are you?"

He and the girls smiled, obviously knowing my mom watched from the front window.

"You really *are* a special one, aren't you? I think you know who we are." He stepped closer to me and stopped, as if there was an invisible line he couldn't cross.

"Why are you here?"

"You've been given something you don't want. Just renounce it and it will go away. Your life will go back to the way it was and you won't have to carry this load anymore. I can only imagine the burden—"

"I don't know what—"

He stepped back and one of the girls stepped forward, continuing his sentence, "—you're carrying—what it's doing to you. It's overwhelming, isn't it?

"It's all a game, really. It's too much for a child though. You can't win. Just live your life…"

"Play video games," the other girl said, stepping forward. "Hang out with your friends. They're oblivious to what's going on in the world anyway, other than video games, selfies, and learning to twerk."

"Ha ha!" Drake laughed. He turned to the side and began twerking. "I've got it. Do I have it?"

"They deserve to be punished," the girl continued.

"Punished?"

"But, if there is anything I can do to help you reach your dreams...," Drake said, taking control of the conversation again. "...I will do it for you. Anything you want. You only need ask. At this very moment, I can put an idea in your head for a business that you can start right now as a kid. It will become very successful, and you can then sell the company for millions. Your family will never want for anything. Just renounce the gift."

"How do I do that?"

The girls looked at each other, pleased, and smiled.

"Say aloud that you don't want the gift. That's it. It's simple. No one will hold it against you. Besides, you won't win."

I backed up one step as he stepped closer, but he paused and stepped back again, away from that invisible border. My expression questioned what had just happened.

"There are rules to this game," he stated in response.

"You came here to hurt me?"

"No, not you. Why would we do a thing like that?" He glanced over at Dingy's house. "Take care of your friends, won't you? There isn't much time."

"Bye, Sheena," they all stated loudly as they turned and walked away from the house.

As they approached the corner, their bodies melded together. It was like watching dark watercolors blend together in a virtual painting. And when they became one, they transformed into the same thing I'd seen outside the window in class that day. The Murk.

I turned to run into the house. My mom stood in the door, trying to look down the street. I was glad she wasn't looking at me because she'd see how freaked out I was. I checked all the locks on the door after she closed it.

"Who was that? It was nice of them to stop by. The boy was cute, but something wasn't right with him. You know the kind of kid that puts on an act in front of parents when secretly he's the leader of a gang or something?"

"Sounds about right," I said as I ran up the stairs.

I paced back and forth in my room, walking fast, not looking where I was going, and almost smacked my head into my bookshelves.

That was the Murk, or part of the Murk—like its avatars or something. It basically just offered me the world if I'd renounce being a gleamer.

My eyes teared up. *It came to my house.* I began breathing quick and hard. *I need to call Nana! No, this is what they want. They want you to freak out,* I told myself. *They wanted to scare you. If they did all of this...* I stopped walking. *There's something about me that they fear!*

Teddy and I were on speaking terms again. Chana convinced me I couldn't stay mad at him forever. It really didn't take much convincing.

Chana and I exchanged stories on what happened when we were in the principal's office and on what happened once we got home. "Are you still alive?" she asked via text, sure my dad had killed me from the way he glanced at her when he left the office. She got into a lot less trouble than I did, probably because Cameron attacked her first.

I entered my closet, pulled the louvered door shut behind me, sat on the closet floor next to my dirty clothes bin, and called Chana. "Look, I'm not supposed to even be on the phone unless it's an emergency." I spoke softly with my mouth against the phone so she could hear me.

"Oh yeah, you're grounded for life. Did Principal Vernon give you the whole 'be a lady' speech?"

"Yeah, he did."

"Well don't listen to him. You're not like the rest of us. You have to think about your destiny. I'll be a lady. You be a legend."

"You're quoting Stevie Nicks? Oh my gosh! That's why you're my best friend." If I'd been at Chana's house, I would have hugged her around the waist and flipped her over onto her pile of pillows as we laughed hysterically.

"Don't be a lady, be a legend." I couldn't believe she knew that quote.

"You need to talk to Theodore."

"Why? He's a traitor."

"It really wasn't his fault. Yes, he was stupid for bringing the journal to school, but Cameron did the damage."

She was right, but I wouldn't tell her that—at least, not right away.

"Now, say you forgive him."

"Nope."

"Stop being difficult. Just say it."

"Nope."

"You're going to end up forgiving him anyway. You might as well say it now."

"Fine. I forgive him."

"No, say, 'I forgive you, Theodore.'"

"I don't call him Theodore, everyone else does."

"Whatever. Say, 'I forgive you, Teddy.'"

I gritted my teeth. "I forgive you, Teddy."

"There, it's done. Now, that wasn't so hard. Did you hear that?"

"Yeah, I did," Teddy replied.

I gasped. "We've been on three-way all this time?"

"Someone had to be the bigger person and get you guys back on track. Besides, you need him."

"Need me for what?"

"Go ahead, Sheena. Tell him what you're planning."

8

I can't believe I'm doing this again, I thought as I snuck out of my house. I gently shut and locked the back door as Teddy rode up on his bike. He leaned it against the back of the house, and I held a finger to my lips and motioned for him to follow me to the wooden shed at the back fence, behind the willow tree. It used to be our clubhouse when we were little.

"Sheesh, how did the three of us ever fit in here with all of our stuff?"

"We were much smaller."

I looked around at the tiny space. "This was a magical place back then, wasn't it?" Chana and I had called the shed our castle sometimes, and we were princesses. We hid in it from the dragon next door which was really a Doberman Pinscher that barked through the fence at us.

"Yeah, magical," Teddy said while fumbling with his jacket pocket. "Does it smell like skunk in here to you?"

"No, it does not. That's moisture."

Teddy pulled notes from his pocket. "Well, moisture smells like skunk. Let's get to work. "How many times did you say you've had the dream with the sludge?"

"Three times."

"Wow, and the dream was exactly the same each time?"

"Exact."

The shed door flung open, and we both gasped as I jumped back into Teddy.

"Hey!"

"Shh…"

"Oops, sorry. Why do you guys look so frightened? You knew I was coming," said Chana.

"I guess it's just that it's dark out and all…" I hadn't told them about my visitors, and hours later, it kind of felt like it didn't really happen.

"Dang, it's kind of tight in here."

"Yeah, just squeeze on in."

"Shh… Did you hear that?" asked Teddy. "Someone's out there."

None of us moved. We looked toward the door, now partially open, at the beam from a flashlight aimed at the ground in front of the door.

My heart pounded wildly. My dad had heard me leave and was going to kill me. How would I explain us being out here? But then I realized we would have heard the drag of his foot from his limp. Maybe it was my mom.

A hand pulled the door back, and one black and white Nike tennis shoe stepped into the entrance of the shed.

"What is he doing here?"

"I invited him," said Chana.

"Why the heck did you do that?" asked Teddy.

"Are you crazy?" I added. "We were just in a fight with him."

"Oh, we cleared all that up."

I couldn't believe what I was hearing. Were all my friends turning on me? I mean, my two friends?

Cameron lifted the bill of his baseball cap so he could see us better, then turned it to the back of his head. "Look, I don't want to be here anymore than you want me here. I can leave."

"Then why did you even agree to it?" Chana asked with her hands on her hips.

"Because what I read in Theodore's diary—"

"It's not a diary," said Teddy.

"—was kind of interesting. And nothing ever happens around here. Plus, you said we would be joining you on a quest. And I was like, why not?"

"An adventure is what I said."

"What's the difference?"

"Wait, we? Who is we?" I asked. Having Cameron there was bad enough, now there was someone else?

For some reason I expected to see Ariel and I was a little happy about it, but Bradly peeked her head in, around Cameron. Her waist length micro-braids fell over her shoulder. "Hey," she said.

I couldn't believe it, the queen of the FPS at my house? "You've got to be kidding me." I turned to Chana. "Why?"

"Because we need backup. Trust me, they're in, and this is going to work."

"My cousins are all set," said Cameron. "I just have to tell them where."

"Your cousins? Even more people are getting involved?" I pushed past them, hitting the shed door, not caring if it slammed back into the wall and woke my parents, and stormed down the drive.

Teddy ran after me and threw a stick at my back.

I spun around. "Why did you do that?"

"I can't yell your name when we're standing under your parent's window. Listen, it's not a bad thing they're here," he whispered.

"They were not part of my plan."

"They were not part of my plan," he repeated, mimicking my voice. "You know you have control issues. There's nothing wrong with a little help."

"What kind of help? Help to put them in danger? Really, none of you should be involved with this. I don't know what I was thinking."

"Well, I don't know what you're thinking now, but it should only be about saving Dingy. That's why we're here, right? It's not about us or our issues with Bradly or Cameron." he grabbed my arm. "Come on, let's hear them out."

"They don't even believe."

"They don't need to. You do. You're the gleamer."

I sucked my teeth.

"Sheena, look, he may not want you to know he believes, but if he didn't, would he really be here?"

As much as I hated to admit it, Teddy had a point. I followed him back to the shed, sulking.

"Alright, they're back. Can we move on now?" asked Chana.

"Okay, tell me the dream again. Let's take this step by step," said Teddy, once we were all squeezed shoulder-to-shoulder inside the shed.

"A dream?" Cameron sighed and looked up at the ceiling.

"Shut it, Cameron," Chana snapped.

Teddy tried to remember what I'd told him earlier. "You went after the guys that stole the stool from you dad..."

"Right. I followed them to a dark building. It was on a campus of some sort."

"I've been searching maps all afternoon, and you were right that it's the projects and not a university campus. The only ones that look like a campus layout are in the Heights."

We all leaned over his phone, looking at the map of the area. I pointed to a spot on the map. "What's that?"

Teddy switched the map to street view. "It's a warehouse. But that's not what you saw, right?"

"No." But there was something about that warehouse that bothered me. Seeing the street view of it gave me chills.

"My cousin lives near there. That's on the edge of the city. A lot of buildings are boarded up over there and that apartment complex is a little dangerous. Are you sure about this?" asked Cameron.

My heart raced a little. "As sure as I'm going to get."

"He's there?"

"He has to be. That's what the dream was about."

"Okay, what happened next, again?" asked Teddy

"There was a black sludge, alive, and worse on different floors—"

"You mean like Aether?" asked Cameron.

We looked at each other.

"Sheesh, you guys need to come outside your bubble sometimes. It's like in the movie—"

Teddy snapped his fingers. "Yeah, now I know what you're talking about, like that."

"So, it's a dark and evil force, then?"

"That's something we're going to have to come up against. Sheena said it was after some kid, and that it was only in that building," said Chana.

Teddy used a flashlight and shined it down on a notepad as he took notes. "Then what happened?"

I continued, "Then the dream switched to Dingy, and the evil guy I had to save him and his family from. I used my body to block—"

"Hold up. See, that right there is the part that makes me not want to do this. I'm concerned about that last part," said Teddy.

"Block what? Let her finish. It's just getting good," said Cameron.

"Your dream was like a whole horror movie, and you were the star. But you never saw the end of the movie, did you?" asked Bradly.

"Why are you here?" I asked, maybe sounding a bit too hostile.

"Because this is creepy, and cool, and I'm pumped."

"Cheerleader."

"Yeah, I am. Proud of it, and living my best life."

"Just stop," said Teddy. "Maybe we should all go home and just rethink this."

"Teddy, we can do this," I said, looking at him and around at everyone else, trying to reassure them—reassure myself, forcing a team player attitude to come forth.

"Why can't we just tell the police?" asked Bradly.

"They won't believe something from a dream."

"No one will."

"Cameron, I've had it. If you don't believe, why are you here?"

"Because of the Bible."

"The Bible?"

Cameron nodded. "In the Book of Acts it says, and I quote, 'In the last days, God says, I will pour out my Spirit on all people. Your sons and daughters will prophesy, your young men will see visions, your old men will dream dreams...'"

"Whoa, how do you know that? You go to church?"

"My dad is a pastor."

"Then why do you act the way you do?"

"There's no way your dad is a pastor," said Teddy.

"Why all the shade? I'm so misunderstood," he said while fake crying.

"I can't believe it."

"So now that you know, can we get back to how we're going to get this kid out of there?"

"You're not, I am," I replied.

"We don't have weapons, and there are gangs over there. You have sight, not superpowers," said Teddy.

"Ha!" Cameron exclaimed. "Didn't your angel give you a weapon to use against the bad guys?"

"I have a guardian angel." It came out before I had a chance to think about it. Maybe it was supposed to be a secret.

"Well, where the heck is he? Is he coming? We couldn't possibly fit one more person in this shed."

Teddy shook his head and rolled his eyes in exasperation. "Did he reveal himself yet?"

"Wow, they're really having this conversation," Bradly whispered to Cameron.

"I think it's my grandmother." *Or Ariel,* I thought, but that would prove itself that night if she appeared.

"Nana?" Chana exclaimed, finally speaking—which made me a little nervous. Chana was never so quiet.

"That doesn't sound right," said Teddy.

"Based on what? What Mr. Tobias told you?"

"Something like that. And, don't think I'm going to tell you what he said just so you won't have an attitude with me about the journal."

"The thought *had* crossed my mind."

"Open the door and let some air in here. It's too stuffy," said Cameron. "Why are we having this conversation in this outhouse-looking shed, anyway?"

"Because my house and everything on this property is protected from evil."

"You believe that?" asked Cameron.

Bradly smirked and pointed at Cameron. "That can't be right, evil is right there."

Cameron played like he would put Bradly in a headlock, although the space was too small.

I stared at him. "It's all a front, isn't it?"

"What?"

"The way you act at school—mean, and all the 'Yo, whaz up baby' talk?" I made motions with my arms as he would as I spoke. "You haven't talked like that since you've been here. You're not that guy, are you?"

Cameron huffed air from his nose as he looked away.

"I get it. The preacher's son has to show he's down."

"You know what—"

"Yeah, I do. I know that this Cameron—the one that's right here, right now—is a likeable person."

Cameron's mouth had been open, to say something, but he closed it. The way he looked at me—I don't know, I can't describe it. I don't think anyone had looked at me like that before, that I'd noticed. My cheeks felt hot. I think I blushed.

Chana watched us and then looked over at Teddy, who was frowning. "Uh, so, what are we doing, Theodore?"

"Let's get going. Chana, you're all set, right?" asked Teddy.

She looked back and forth at us. "Yeah, let's just go. All of you are giving me a headache. You guys head out. We'll leave a half hour behind you."

"And you know what to say if you get caught, right?"

"We've got it, just go."

Cameron pushed the door, but it didn't budge. "What's wrong with this door?"

"Are we locked in?" asked Bradly.

"No, it's probably just stuck." I pushed the door with my foot, but it didn't move. It was like someone had rolled a boulder in front of it.

"Could someone have locked us in?" asked Teddy.

"No, there's no way," said Chana. "That lock rusted off years ago, didn't it, Sheena?"

"Yeah, it did."

Teddy and Cameron ran the lights from their flashlights over the door as Chana and I pushed.

"Did something fall in front of the door?" asked Bradly, her voice beginning to quiver.

"You just walked in here, did you see anything out there other than a tree?"

"No, but—"

"Listen, do you hear that?"

Something whipped around outside of the shed.

The whole shed began to shake.

We all fell back against the back wall and into each other.

"It's an earthquake!" Teddy yelled.

But I knew it wasn't.

The woodshed was anchored to a concrete slab. The whole slab lifted into the air and slammed back down. That wasn't the worst part. The worst part was the sound coming from outside and the shaking of the walls, to the point that the wood panels began to pull apart. The wind howled and we heard what sounded like millions of wings flapping.

"What the heck is happening?" yelled Bradly as we huddled together.

"Get under the table," yelled Cameron.

"Only one of us can fit under there."

"Well, get down."

We all knelt.

Chana put her arm through mine. She looked like she was trying to hold back from screaming. I looked around at my terrified friends, Bradly in tears, Teddy and Cameron with their eyes squeezed shut and hands covering their ears to block out the sound.

I pulled away from Chana, stood, and faced the door.

"Sheena, what are you doing?" yelled Teddy.

The Murk didn't want them, it wanted me. I pushed at the door, ready to face what was out there if it meant protecting my friends.

The door opened this time and as soon as it did, silence fell around us. I stepped outside, followed by Cameron, with his fists raised as if he were going to fight someone. There was no indication that what we just experienced had even happened. The ground wasn't overturned, the willow limbs were still, and Teddy's bike was still against my house.

"I don't get it. What was that?" asked Teddy.

"A warning. Now I really know I have to do this. You guys... I appreciate the help, but this isn't your fight, and I don't want you in danger. So, if you want to back out, I totally get it."

"You know I'm with you no matter what," Chana said as she grabbed my hand and squeezed.

"You know you aren't going anywhere without me," Teddy said as he grabbed onto Chana's hand.

Cameron stood back with his hands on his hips, staring at the shed. "I've come this far, I might as well see it through to the end. You're going to need some muscle anyway, since

Theodore is such a punk." He smirked at him and placed his hand on top of ours. "Brad-Boogie?"

"I'm sorry, I can't," said Bradly, while backing away toward the driveway. "This is too much for me."

I don't think I'd ever heard her voice sound so tiny.

"Thank you, Bradly. Thank you for being honest," I replied.

"You can go home, but you can't tell anyone about this—ever, Ms. Team player," said Chana.

"She's not going anywhere. Get your hand in here."

"No, Cameron. Let her go."

"Bradly, do not vlog about this," said Chana.

She didn't respond.

"She won't," Cameron whispered. "Can't you see how shaken up she is"

We all watched Bradly leave, her head hanging low and her arms hugging herself.

As I got my bike and headed to the driveway, I looked up at the house at the picture window. A dark figure stood, watching. I waited, holding my breath, but nothing happened. No one charged out of the house to stop me or came into full view so I could see who or what it was. So, I turned around the side of the house, and it turned, watching me.

Looking back at the house, I almost rammed my bike into Chana.

"What's wrong?"

"Sheena, I need to talk to you. I need to tell you something."

9

*C*hana ran her fingers through the curls at the nape of her neck like she often did when she was deep in thought.

"What's wrong? Are you okay?"

"Yes, come here."

She hugged me. I mean, she hugged me like she thought she'd never see me again.

I pushed her away. "What are you doing? You're making it seem like this is the end of our lives or something."

"I won't let anything happen to you," Chana replied.

"Why did you say that? Did you have a premonition or something?"

Chana tried to smile. "Just remember that no matter what it seems, you're not alone." She bumped her fists, crossed her arms above her and brought them down. I returned our bestie gesture and watched her walk away and then jog to catch up to Cameron.

"What was that about?" asked Teddy, riding back toward me.

"Everybody is worried."

"Are you?"

"I don't know."

The night was oddly quiet, other than the clicking sound of our bicycle wheels spinning over the road. And it was darker than usual. Teddy didn't seem to notice, so I rode close to him down Peck Street, which took us straight into the Heights.

Muskegon Heights is south of Muskegon. You really wouldn't know when you left one city and entered the next, but as kids we always wanted to go to the Heights. It just seemed like the kids there were up on whatever was new: styles, music, everything.

For once, I didn't feel like I was being watched. But why didn't I? Shouldn't the Murk be watching me or doing something more to try to stop me? There was not even as much as a warning text from the angel to say 'thou shalt not go there' or something like that.

I spoke too soon. I stopped my bike in the middle of the street. Teddy was about twenty feet away before he noticed I wasn't with him.

He looked back over his shoulder and jumped off his bike, allowing it to fall to the ground, and ran back to me.

Lightning flashed in the sky behind him and lowered toward the ground. In that flick of light, I saw the Murk expanding and swirling around. Then they were just there—the three teens, at the end of the block, the boy in the middle and the two girls behind him on either side. He looked at me with his head cocked to the side, his hands clasped together behind him.

"Sheena, don't look at it. Look at me."

But I couldn't tear my eyes away from it.

"You're focusing on the wrong thing."

A wave of fear crashed over me like a Tsunami. I couldn't escape it. I was drowning.

"I can't-I can't do this, Teddy. I don't know what I was thinking. I'm just a kid. No, I don't want to do this. I just want to go home."

"You don't want to go home. Don't listen to them, Sheena."

The Murk guy, Drake, nodded. Then I nodded. "Yes, I do. I want to go home."

"You want to go, and forget about Dingy? Sheena, look at me."

Teddy grabbed my shoulders and shook me.

"Yes, we need to go back. I don't want to do this."

Teddy stood directly in front of me and lowered his head into my face. "This isn't you. This is them. You're listening to their fear. You have to fight, Sheena."

I finally looked in his eyes. They were beginning to tear.

"I can't fight. I don't know how to fight. I don't want to fight." My words seemed to come from a faraway place. I was sinking deeper.

"You're not going to help Dingy?"

"I-I can't."

"You don't have to, I will," Teddy said as he turned, mumbling his displeasure in what was happening. He ran back to his bike, jumped on, and pedaled away.

I remained in the street, transfixed by the Murk.

A battle went on inside my head. *Turn around and go home. Teddy's leaving. You can't help them. Them? Who is them? Teddy needs you. I have nothing to do with this.* I turned my bike and began riding back home as the torment continued in my head.

My legs pedaled faster. I had to get home. I drove right through an intersection. A car horn blared as a vehicle came close to hitting me. I swerved to the side and into a parked car.

I landed with a thud on the trunk and rolled off onto the ground. My head began to throb. I squeezed my eyes shut for a moment and took a deep breath.

I don't know if it was me swaying back and forth or the inside of my head as I picked up my bike and started pedaling again. A tear fell from my eye. *You're so close, Sheena,* I heard in my head. *That's why they're trying to stop you.*

Go home, a voice said in my head. It was my voice, but not my tone or words.

"No!" I yelled and squeezed the brake levers on the handlebars. I turned my bike, ignoring what I saw in front of me and the overpowering battle in my head, and charged up the street. My mom always says do it scared if you must but do it. I rode right through the Murk, while letting out a sharp cry. I didn't look back as I sailed through the intersection. Thank God there were no cars coming this time.

"Teddy!"

He slowed, allowing me to catch up.

He looked in my eyes. "You're back. I can see it. It's a good thing too. I don't even know what I'm looking for."

"But that wasn't going to keep you from trying..."

"I hoped it would snap you out of it."

I studied him. "What else did Mr. Tobias tell you?"

"That the Murk would try to get in your head. Sheena, they have no more power than you give them. Fear is their main weapon."

I smiled at him. "Thank you for being my friend, Teddy."

"Girl, you're seriously going to make me rethink that," he said with a laugh. "Are we good now?"

"Yeah, they're gone."

"But watching, right?"

"Or scheming, or both."

We rode our bikes for another couple of miles. Teddy pointed at a convenience store and pulled into its parking lot.

"What are you doing? Why are you stopping?"

"I need something to drink."

"Right now? Really? You have to have a pop right now?"

"I would prefer an Oreo shake, but they won't have that. An orange pop will have to do."

"Oh, that's right. You're a nervous eater."

"I'm not nervous. We're almost there, and I just need something to drink."

As Teddy lifted his leg over his bike, a man with a grocery bag exited the store and walked toward a black Lexus.

He glanced over at us and did a double take. "Sheena? Theodore? What are you doing out here at this time of night?"

What were *we* doing there? What was Principal Vernon doing there? This is what I meant about Muskegon being a small town and having to be careful because if you're doing something wrong, you either run into someone who knows your family, or they will reprimand you themselves like they're your family.

I glanced over at Teddy, not sure of what to say.

"Just going to the store, Mr. Vernon," Teddy replied.

Principal Vernon looked at his car and back at us. He held a finger up to someone in the car and walked toward me, shifting his bag from his right arm to his left.

"Sheena…" he glanced over at Teddy and lowered his voice. "That's my wife in the car. How did you know—"

"I saw it."

"How could you?"

"You showed me."

Principal Vernon frowned. He didn't understand. "How did you know about my wife? Her illness? I mean, I didn't even know."

"No matter how many times you ask, the answer doesn't change. I saw it."

"I don't know what that means. I'm confused about…" He rubbed his forehead with his free hand. "Am I to believe you have some kind of ability, or gift?"

"I can't tell you what to believe, sir, but, umm…we need to get home. See you at school."

We pedaled away from the store. When I looked back, Principal Vernon was still standing in the same spot, watching us.

"Oh my gosh, that was close. What was he talking about?" asked Teddy.

I made sure I didn't do the face thing that gives away that I'm lying. "Nothing. Let's hurry."

We stood down the block from the apartment complex, looking over the grounds. My eyes drifted to the warehouse beyond it. "They sure don't have much lighting out here. Someone could easily hide and jump out and grab you."

"Not a thought we need to have right now. Which building is it?"

I closed my eyes, picturing a scene from the dream. "Um, okay, there's this kid—around sixteen. He's light-skinned and has braids." I squeezed my eyes shut. "No, funny looking ponytails."

"No, they're called freeform locs, and he has stripes down his sleeves, right?" Teddy asked.

"How do you know that?"

"He's right there."

I gasped. *The exact scene from my dream.* The guy on the sidewalk, wearing a black bomber jacket with writing on it, talking to some other guys around the same age that leaned against a car.

Okay, okay, this is happening. Just like my dream. That means everything else in my dream is going to happen. Like, literal. I began breathing heavily and rolled my bike back a few feet. *Stay calm, girl,* I thought. *You're so close.* That's what I'd heard in my head earlier. Was that the angel encouraging me? As if to say don't give up now?

Nana would tell me not to let my emotions get the best of me. *Yes, I know, Nana. What would Nana do right now?* I closed my eyes and lifted my head. A breeze blew over it, lifting my curls away from my face and off my shoulders. A chill ran through me.

"What are you doing? Moon bathing?" asked Teddy.

"Shh..."

Teddy came closer. "Who were you talking to?"

"The wind."

Even with my eyes closed, I knew he looked at me just like I would've looked at him, had he said the same thing.

"The wind? You do that now? No, what I want to know is why you need to do that?"

"You have no idea what's about to happen—worse than the mind games I went through back there. This is dimensional warfare. We need help."

"From the wind?"

"No, from angels. I'm just putting in a request."

"Did you tell it to blow those guys away?"

"We don't need to worry about them. What we need right now is for the four winds to change direction."

"Great, now you're talking in riddles like Mr. Tobias."

I opened my eyes. There was no time to explain. "Come on. Act like we know where we're going."

"Do we?" He watched me pass him. "I mean, you do, right?"

As we rolled our bikes past the guys near the corner, I could feel their eyes on me. *Just let us by, just let us by,* I thought over and over.

"Hey!" one of them said.

I looked back. Another guy turned his hand palm-down at his neck and waved it back and forth, as if to tell him not to do whatever he was thinking of doing.

That was a relief.

We stepped in front of the walkway that led to Building A. I stopped, feeling like I'd hit a brick wall.

"What's wrong?" asked Teddy.

"Noth-nothing." It was hard to get the word out. My lungs weren't cooperating. "I'm getting the same feeling from the dream."

"This must be it, then." Teddy looked around. "Those guys are watching us. Maybe we should go inside. Let's take the bikes inside the hallway."

Teddy held the door as I rolled my bike in and leaned it against the wall. I held it in turn for him, looked up the stairs, and down the dim hall at the grey stained carpet, almost black down the center. There were four doors at the end of the hall, two on either side.

"Okay, in your dream you were upstairs. I think we need to check out one floor at a time. We should've had another plan for once we got inside," said Teddy, after chaining our bikes together. He handed me the suitcase he'd strapped on the back of his bike.

"No, you stay here. This part I have to do alone."

"Sheena, don't start. You know I would not have let you go through with this if I were going to let you do it alone."

"But in the dream, I was by myself. I have to do it alone."
I said it like I had all the courage in the world, even though
my legs were shaking.

"The dream showed you what was happening. It didn't
mean you were supposed to come here. I keep telling you
that."

"Yeah, but no one would believe me, so I have to find
him. Dingy doesn't have much time, Teddy. I can feel it."

"Okay then, let's find him." Teddy started cautiously up
the stairs. "I don't know what I'm looking for until you tell
me, so I'm just winging it."

"Sheesh, why are you so difficult?" I climbed the stairs
behind him. "We're going up to the next to the top floor."

With each level we reached, my chest tightened until it
felt like it was being squeezed in a vice. It was everything.
The air felt heavy, there was a grey hue over everything that
only I could see, and the feeling, like we were walking
through a dark, evil place.

'This is the floor," I whispered. I couldn't speak any
louder than that if I tried. I pointed down the hall, and
Teddy followed me to a door.

"Any sign of the Murk?"

"No."

"Good. He's in there?" he whispered.

"He's in a metal room."

"Like a panic room? You didn't say anything about that
before. How in the world are we supposed to get him out

of a panic room?" Teddy's voice rose, and the apartment door swung open.

10

"*¡Hola!*" I said.

The woman stared at us. There were dark patches under her eyes, and frizzy auburn hair hung from beneath a red bandana.

I began speaking Spanish as fast as I could—everything I'd learned in class.

She looked confused. "Who are you looking for? You have the wrong apartment," she said with a raspy voice, and tried to close the door while holding a cigarette between her fingers.

Teddy pushed the door and spoke in Spanish also. Except, his Spanish was so bad. No wonder he needed a tutor. Why he told her the insect is small and the cheese is in the water, I have no idea. But it was enough for us to keep talking and push our way inside the apartment like we thought we were supposed to be there.

"James, get down here," the woman said into her phone. She held up a finger to us. "Wait. Uh, una mometa, porvari."

Teddy looked at me as if to say, *what did she say?*

"*Un momento, por favor.*"

"*Ah, sí,*" he replied, nodding.

"That's what I meant," the woman replied smugly.

I looked around the apartment and noticed a huge map of the United States on the wall of what should've been a dining area. It looked more like a messy office. Instead of a table and chairs, there was a folding card table stacked with papers, boxes on the floor, and next to the door, a wall of file cabinets. Red tipped stick pins stuck out of the map on the states of Michigan, Ohio, Illinois, Georgia, and Florida.

The scent of stale cigarettes and bacon lingered in the air, mixed with a scent that I knew to mean 'take the stinky trash outside to the bin before you get in trouble for acting like you don't notice it.'

We could hear feet bounding down the stairs. James ran into the apartment as if he were chasing someone and came to an abrupt stop when he saw us.

"What's this?" he asked with his hands on his hips. He had spiky hair and looked normal compared to the haggard woman.

Teddy looked at me as if to ask if that was the guy—the kidnapper.

I shook my head.

"I believe they're lost." The woman smirked as she closed the door behind him. "They're looking for someone, and they have luggage with them. I think they were given the wrong address."

She spit something out to the side onto the linoleum floor. *Yuck!*

"Can you imagine," she added with a wicked laugh, revealing nicotine stained teeth and a missing tooth on the left side. "It brought them here, of all places."

James walked toward me. "What's your name, girly?"

Teddy's arm, against mine, tensed. If he tried to defend me, or came across as aggressive, we could be in real trouble. Not that we weren't already. We had one chance to get this right. I grasped his hand with my fingers just for a moment, hoping it would tell him to calm down.

"*¿Qué?*" I looked at the woman for help.

"She doesn't understand. They don't speak English."

James laughed and spun around. "You've got to be kidding me."

The woman leaned forward in my face. "You don't know how unlucky you are right now.

"Look at them, they're totally green, too."

I smiled, reached my hand out, and placed my palm on the side of her face.

It was just like what happened with Principal Vernon. A door opened behind her eyes, and I saw what was on the other side.

"She likes you," said James. "Good. Take them back with the others. You need help?"

She stepped back, waving for us to follow her down the hall. "With these two? No, I think I can handle them. Plus, my Spanish is better than yours. Comeo thiso wayo."

"Good, I'm going to let Luke know. He'll be excited about this. Maybe it'll get his attention off that flipping wall for a bit. Ha! We don't have to take them, they're coming to *us* now."

I gave Teddy a look that said, *did you catch what he just said?*

He glanced at me, which was enough to let me know he did.

We followed the woman down a narrow hall to a room behind a room where she unlocked and opened a steel door.

"Right in there," she said with a perky tone.

I stepped into the dark room but wouldn't budge from the entrance even when pushed. I needed my eyes to adjust. *You've got to be here,* I thought.

As my eyes adjusted, I saw that the room was no larger than a walk-in closet. Rusted metal walls surrounded us. It was like standing inside of a tall dumpster. There was a clump of something in the corner. It looked like a pile of dirty pajamas. A kid looked up, but it wasn't Dingy. Another kid sat up. I think they'd huddled together to comfort each other. The kid behind her didn't budge.

"*¿Qué es esto?*" I asked the woman. I said it loudly hoping the kid in the back would hear me and recognize my voice.

The girl in front of him started crying.

"Get in there," the woman said, now in a harsher tone.

The boy turned. As soon as he did, *thwack!*

Teddy brought his head back as hard as he could, butting the woman behind him in the nose.

"Sheena!" Dingy exclaimed and ran at me, wrapping his arms around my waist.

"Ah, crap!" she cried out from under her hands, covering her mouth and nose as she fell back. Her phone fell from her and Teddy kicked it away.

"I knew you'd find me."

"How did you know?"

"I wished it," Dingy replied.

Teddy held his head. "That hurt."

The woman groaned as she tried to rise.

"Grab her!" yelled Teddy.

We pushed her into the room, locking her in as there wasn't a knob on the other side.

"I can't believe your plan worked. What are we going to do about that James guy?"

"Maybe he'll stay wherever that Luke person is," I replied.

"I'm scared," said one of the kids.

I leaned forward in front of them. "I need you guys to be brave. Just like I am, okay? Can you do that for me?"

I couldn't believe I'd just said that. I was freaking out inside.

Dingy nodded with frightened eyes.

"Let's get out of here," said Teddy.

"What's upstairs? Do you know what's upstairs?" I asked the kids.

They shook their heads and held on tight to my arms.

"Okay, don't worry. We're going to get you to your parents."

"My mommy is looking for me," said the little girl.

"They were going to take us to a farm," Dingy announced.

"A farm?" My mind flashed to the map on the wall in the dining room.

"Let's just get out of here," said Teddy.

We ran through the apartment, and then slowly opened the door, making sure no one was in the hall.

"Go," I whispered and motioned for Teddy and the kids to head out in front of me.

A really awful feeling came over me, and I fought against the terror of it. Something wasn't right. Everything played out much too easily, compared to the dream.

Teddy ran down the stairs with the kids. At the next landing, he put his arm out, stopping them as he looked down the hall to make sure it was clear.

I watched them over the banister, looking out for that James guy, relieved they'd soon be out of the building. At least if they kept going, and he came from upstairs, he'd have to get past me, not that I had any idea what I'd do. They only had to make it down four more floors.

As I watched, the area around me seemed to grow darker, as if I were viewing everything through a tunnel, but the hall light hadn't dimmed.

The hairs on my arms stood on end. Something was behind me, but I couldn't make myself turn to see what it was. *Don't be afraid,* I told myself. *The Murk is just trying to put more fear in you.* My body shook so hard, my curls were jiggling. *Calm down, calm down,* I told myself, but it wasn't working.

I held tightly to the banister as I was grabbed from behind and lifted off the floor. "Now where do you think you're going?" the voice asked, wrapping around me and tightening like chains.

He tried to drag me back, but I wouldn't let go of the railing as I struggled.

"Sheena!" Teddy yelled, looking up over the rail from below.

"Keep going," I yelled after him. I could see part of a body running up from below, toward them, that looked like James. "He's coming!" I yelled.

The guy peeled my fingers from the rail and spun me around, knocking me into the wall. He held me there, looking into my face. There were black smudges on his face and hands, and red blotches.

"Where have I seen you before? I know you, don't I?"

His face flashed back and forth from that of a man to the sludge I dreamed about. Yes, he had seen me. He was the man in that truck whose eyes flashed red. I guess he was Luke.

I struggled to get out of his grasp.

He held my face with one hand, turn my head from side to side, and grinned. "Yeah, I know you. You've been haunting me."

Me, haunting him? Is he serious?

"They sent you, didn't they?"

They? I didn't know who he was talking about.

"You're trying to ruin everything I've built here. Come, let me show you what's upstairs."

"No!" I yelled and tried to fight. Whatever happened, he was not taking me up those stairs.

He froze for a moment, hearing running and then a scuffle coming from a few flights below. Men were yelling. Then feet were bounding up toward us.

He flung me off to the side and ran up the stairs.

Principal Vernon and some of the guys that had been out on the sidewalk when we arrived ran up the stairs toward me.

"You okay?" The kid with the freeform locs asked.

"Yes," I replied, as he helped me up from the floor.

"This is my cousin," said Cameron, joining them. "His friends are down there with the guy that attacked Theodore. Sheena, they got him. The kids are safe."

"The police are on the way," said Principal Vernon. "I knew something was up. Theodore had a suitcase on the back of his bike. I thought either you two were running away to get married, or one of you was running away from home, so I followed you."

I should've said thank you or asked if Teddy was injured or where Chana was, because my mind went to those places. But what came out was, "I have to go after him. We can't let him get away."

"I can't let you do that," said Principal Vernon. "The police can handle it from here."

"He's heading for the back stairwell. I know where he's going."

Cameron angled his head toward the back wall and flashed his eyes to the left.

He's trying to tell me something...

"Mr. Vernon is right— *Oof!*" Cameron exclaimed as he tripped up the last step and fell toward Principal Vernon, giving me an opportunity to jet around him and up the stairs.

"Sheena!" Principal Vernon yelled. He didn't move quick enough to stop me.

I ran up the stairs and stopped at the top. A door at the far end closed from someone just running out.

I took in everything around me. The area wasn't fit for anyone to live in. It looked more like a storage area. There were no walls separating the space where two apartments should've been. Maybe it was under construction.

My breath caught in my chest, noticing the wall to my right, illuminated by two work lights aimed up from the floor. Then I noticed the ladder, paint cans, and the paint on the floor. This is why his hands were stained black and red. On the wall was a huge mural—of my face.

Principal Vernon ran in. "Oh my god, what is this?" he said, staring at the wall. He waved his arms toward me. "Sheena, come back this way. I smell gas."

I sniffed the air. He was right. It didn't stop me, though. I ran across the room and out the back door, following the man.

11

L uke, or whoever he was, needed to be caught, but how in the world did I think *I* was going to catch him? I had already done what I planned, which was to find Dingy, but I couldn't break loose of the dream. There was more. The frightening part where I tried to save the group of kids by throwing my body in front of them, shielding them from the bad guy.

And that was why that warehouse up the road bothered me so much. The rest of the dream didn't take place in the apartment complex, but in that warehouse. I was certain of it.

Out on the back stairwell, I looked in the direction of the warehouse, hoping to see Luke running or something.

Mr. Vernon looked down from the door, yelling my name. There were no lights, so I hoped he couldn't see me race across the dirt lawn.

I ran to the back end of the complex, climbed over the chain-link fence, and jumped down as police sirens approached behind me, pulling up to the apartment building.

The warehouse was like a monster growing before me, large and frightening, and I had no idea how I was going to get inside.

Everywhere I looked, there were wood pallets stacked up as tall as me. They surrounded me like a fortress. I squeezed around them to the back of the warehouse where a grey metal door was cracked open. I stood there for a moment. *Did he leave it open for me? Did he know I would follow?* I looked behind me but saw no one.

My hand slowly pulled the door open just wide enough for me to enter, and I was careful to not allow it to slam shut behind me. I left it slightly open just as he had, in case I needed to make a quick escape.

A dimly lit corridor stretched several feet before me.

You're here now, Sheena. What are you going to do? I asked myself. What could I do, but keep going? I felt something pulling me to continue on.

Each step I took felt like my final steps toward the edge of a cliff before jumping off.

There wasn't a sound coming from anywhere until I got further down the hall and approached what appeared to be rows of offices on either side of the corridor. Overhead, fluorescent lights buzzed as they flickered and shut off. I wished I'd brought a flashlight, and then remembered my phone. I shined the light into the window of one of the rooms but didn't see anything.

For a moment, I doubted what I was doing there. Then my thoughts went from bad to worse.

Forget this. Turn around and leave. You're just a kid. This is too much. There's nothing you can do. You're not strong enough. Life would be easier if...

STOP!

You're going to die...

Were the walls closing in on me, or was I just imagining it?

The Murk started another battle in my mind. That had to mean I was getting closer. But close to what? My hands clasped the sides of my head and I shrieked *"NO,"* inside my head.

I leaned forward, catching my breath as the thoughts subsided. A hand slapped against the window opposite me, causing me to jump up onto the opposite window.

I gasped as I watched a young girl's face appear in the window. She was around my age, with blonde hair and sad eyes. She held a finger to her lips and pointed up above us.

I nodded, believing she was saying that Luke was upstairs.

Then she disappeared for a minute. When she returned there were about eight more kids with her.

She put her hands together as if she were praying and then made a twisting motion with her hand, trying to tell me I needed a key. One of the other kids blew on the glass. It fogged up and he drew arrows showing me where to go.

I pointed down the hall, and he nodded.

At the end of the hall was an open door on my right, like the kid had drawn. I shined the light from my phone over the walls of the small office, looking for a hook that might hold keys, and then over the papers sprawled over the desk next to a computer monitor. A chart caught my eye. I ran my finger down a column, reading some of the names:

Bear Lake Orchard

Stribling Orchard

Art Orchard

Peach Groves

Urbane Farms

Sweetview Farm

The next column listed how many laborers were transported and the cost for each group.

What is going on? I thought as I rested my hand over a lump under the stack of papers. I carefully lifted the pages and grabbed the single key attached to a metal ring.

I raced back down the hall, unlocking all the rooms. About thirty kids piled out behind me. It was all done in total silence. None of the kids said a word. It must have been a rule that if they made a sound something would happen to them.

I wanted to go back the way I'd come in, but a boy frantically shook his head and pointed forward. I shook my head, but he pointed around at all the kids and then forward again. I assumed he was trying to tell me there were more of them.

We approached the loading dock and knelt, hearing the rolling doors going up. I held my hand up and motioned for them to stay down. I handed the boy the key, then ran up behind bins of apples and looked over them.

Luke walked behind his truck, and I ran off to another area where I could get a better look at what he was doing. He moved fast, like he was in a hurry to get out of there.

"You know I can see you, right?" He yelled, while throwing something into the bed of the truck. "I can look through muddy water and spot dry land. Ha! My father used to say that."

I held my breath and froze in a squatted position behind a column. I looked back where the kids were. I couldn't see them, so he had to be talking to me. I slowly stood. "It's over."

"It is for you. They know what to do. They will stay quiet in their cages until I return..." He paced for a moment and pounded the sides of his head with his fists. "...when all of this clears up. I'm going to lock you in here with them to keep them fed."

He pointed at his chest. "They're my payload. I supply them to farms up and down the East Coast."

"Why?"

"Why? Ha! Okay, I'll tell you. It's not going anywhere anyway. Labor. Don't worry. It's a win-win situation. They receive a place to sleep and meals in exchange for their labor, and the farms don't have a payroll. They pay me for supplying the workers. And they pay well."

"Why kids?"

"They have endless energy and can work hard for years." He closed the tailgate of the truck. "Now that you know, see you in a few weeks. You'll find everything you need back there."

The kids came out of their hiding places and stood behind me.

"What are you doing out?" He exclaimed.

"We're not staying here. They're all going home, and we're going to find the ones you already sent away."

"We'll see about that," he said as he climbed into his truck. He turned the ignition and revved the engine. Fleetwood Mac's "Landslide" blared from the radio.

Stevie Nicks! Was that a coincidence? Was someone trying to tell me something? *This space is huge*, I thought. *If I run, he'll chase me. I just need to lure him away, so the kids can make a run for it.*

So that's what I did. I ran off to the right and he turned, speeding toward me.

I'd never thought of what it would feel like diving onto a bin of apples. I'm glad I did it without thinking, because it was not like diving onto a bin of marshmallows (not that I knew what that felt like, either).

I rolled over the side and onto the floor. There was no time to think about the pain, I had to keep moving. He kept coming at me until he had me cornered. There was nowhere to run.

The truck raced toward me, and all I knew was that I'd done all I could to save these kids, and just like in the dream, I was willing to throw myself in front of them and block off whatever was coming.

I lifted my hands to my face as the vehicle approached, accepting my fate, just like what almost happened in the alley that day.

CRASH!

The explosive thwack of metal hitting metal attacked my ears. I dropped my hands and stood there, stunned for a minute, before running over to the truck that had slammed into Luke's truck through the opened roller door.

"Chana, are you okay?" I was so happy to see her. "How are you here?"

"I'm okay. We have that tracker thing on our phones, remember? I thought he was getting away. I floored it. I didn't even see you until we were inside. Is he dead?"

"I don't think so. His airbag deployed. You stole your dad's truck?"

"I didn't steal it. I just borrowed it."

"He's going to hate he taught you how to drive a stick shift."

"Yeah well, it's not the worst thing I've done."

"Yes. It is."

"I know, right?"

"You can sit up now, Bradly."

Bradly came forward from the back seat. "I can't believe we just did that."

"You're the one that yelled out, 'Let the big dogs eat!' That means floor it."

"No, I didn't. You did," said Bradly.

"Chana!" I called, breaking up their argument. I mean, really? Who cares who yelled out something about big dogs?

"She changed her mind about joining us," said Chana.

"Yeah, it was just a moment of weakness." Bradly looked around me. "Un-uh, why is Principal Vernon here? We're going to get expelled."

"Where?" asked Chana.

"He just came from back there." Bradly pointed.

"It's okay. Calm down."

The kids all ran toward the truck as police cars pulled up outside. Officers ran in, pulling Luke from the passenger side of his truck.

His face was bloody. I couldn't tell if the blood came from his nose or mouth. He spoke as if he had a swollen tongue as he stated in my direction, "You think it's over? It's not. They're not done with you."

"What's he talking about?" asked Chana.

"I don't know, and I don't care."

A laugh erupted from him. "May your vision be true!"

I froze in place, wide-eyed. How did he know about that?

The police were saying something to him as he struggled with them. For a moment, every sound was blocked from my hearing. Black specks rose from all around the room into the air. They floated up and toward the ceiling where they came together, forming a swirling dust cloud.

Chana shook me, trying to break my stare as the cloud took on a greenish hue, as if decaying, and shot through the ceiling, writhing like a dragon-serpent.

"Let me go! What am I doing here? What happened?" Luke yelled, as if he wasn't the same person that had caused all of this.

That's when I was sure of who he was. "Tobias!" I yelled.

He fell silent and stopped fighting the police.

"Luke Tobias!

He looked in my direction.

"They killed your father."

"What?" he screamed. "Why are you saying that?"

"You renounced your gift, didn't you? They've used you ever since and killed your father."

"No!" Luke yelled. He sobbed loudly as he was taken away.

I knew who he was as soon as he said he could see through muddy water and spot dry land. Mr. Tobias was the only person I'd ever heard say that.

<hr />

There were kids everywhere; some crying happy tears, others hugging, some with police officers.

Principal Vernon looked around the warehouse at everyone with an astonished look on his face, hugging a girl to his side.

"Sheena, those are the twins, Charmayne and Chuck, that were missing," said Chana.

"You did it, Sheena."

"No, we did it." I turned away from Chana, closed my eyes, and whispered, "Thank you."

12

It wasn't easy explaining to the police how I knew where Dingy was—not that I thought it would be. Thank goodness my mom answered the phone and not my dad when the police called. I think she'd been up waiting for the call. She backed me up, although she was not happy about what I'd done.

Chana, Teddy, Cameron, Bradly, and I had already worked out what we'd say. The simplest response (and the key was to keep it simple) was that I recognized the truck when I was in the area, and decided to check it out and make sure it was the same truck from the almost-kidnapping of Ariel before I told anyone.

"At that time of night?" asked the officer.

"Yes, sir. I know that wasn't smart."

"No, it wasn't. You can't go around playing detective. You were lucky this time."

Then I had to explain why my friends were there. That part was easy. Peer pressure.

"So, you talked them into sneaking out of their homes and going with you?"

"Yes, sir. So that I wouldn't be out at night alone. I'm kind of good at talking people into things." I glanced over at my mom and then down at my lap.

My mom placed her hand over mine. "She may not think things through sometimes, but she isn't a liar."

It worked. The others didn't have any answers other than I asked them to go with me. But who could really argue with us when there were so many kids that were able to go home to their families, Luke was behind bars, and they now had a lead on the children that were still missing?

And the pièce de résistance was that Dingy was fine, although he hadn't been fed much other than apples. Luke had planned to transport him and nineteen others the next day to a farm in Florida for strawberry picking, the kids had said. The others were going to another farm.

I still couldn't get over the way Dingy's mom said he'd been taken. It was just the craziest thing. She and Dingy were leaving the supermarket. They walked through the parking lot to their SUV, and Dingy ran around to the passenger side. His mom couldn't see him. She called out to him as she loaded bags in the car, but he didn't answer.

Just that quickly, he'd been taken. Who would've thought that could happen?

I was just glad for it all to be over.

"I guess you don't question who you are anymore?" my mom asked once we were alone.

"I have a lot of questions still, but for the most part I know who I am—for today," I laughed. "A grounded gleamer."

"And, oh how grounded you are," my mom replied without returning my laugh.

<hr />

I fell into the deepest sleep of my life that night, or should I say morning? Every time awoke, I went right back to sleep. Even when my mom tried to get me to eat, I wouldn't. I turned over and went back to sleep. I was drained physically—my body didn't want to move; mentally—I couldn't think anymore; and emotionally—a night of intense feelings ranging from suspicion, to fear, to anger, to empathy, to joy, had left me numb.

When I finally fully awoke, rolled over onto my back, and stared up at the ceiling, the cuts and bruises from my acts of vigilante heroism ached and throbbed like crazy. I think I even felt it in my sleep.

I looked over at the clock on the nightstand to my left and realized two things. First, I'd slept into the next night, and second, I wasn't in my bedroom.

Where am I? I sat up and looked around the room. There was a white lace doily on the nightstand under the clock and over the top of the reclining rocking chair near the window.

Nana.

My mom had taken me to Nana's house instead of home. That way we wouldn't have to explain all of this to my dad. He was asleep when my mom left, and the reports mentioned nothing about a kid getting involved with the rescue. The news reporter only said the police received tips that led to the suspect.

I checked my phone. Not one missed call or text. That meant Chana and Teddy were really in trouble.

The bedroom door squeaked as I opened it and I tiptoed into the bathroom wearing one of Nana's gowns. I jumped when I went back to the bedroom. Nana was sitting in the chair by the window. I hadn't even heard her pass by the bathroom.

"You finally woke up."

"Yes, ma'am."

"How do you feel, sugar?"

"I feel okay."

"Can I get you something to eat?"

"No, thank you."

She pointed next to the bed. "There's water right there."

I didn't realize I was so thirsty. I gulped down the whole glass.

"I felt the wind shift last night. You spoke to it, didn't you?" Nana said with a smile.

I placed the glass back on the stand. "Yes, ma'am. I didn't know what else to do."

"You did what you knew to do. It is only what you know that can save you."

Where had I heard that before? Nurse Javan.

Nana lifted her right hip as she took something out of her pocket. "Sheena, what's this?"

She uncrumpled the wad of paper. "Your mother found it in your pocket. Your clothes are in the dryer, by the way."

I knew what it was, but I walked over to her and looked at it anyway.

"It was on the desk where I found the key to let the kids out at the warehouse."

"Why did you take it?"

"Because of something I saw when I touched it."

"What did you see?"

I sat down at the foot of the bed. "Nana, I don't believe those are farms Luke was sending those kids to."

"Go on..."

"This is going to sound weird because I have no proof..."

"Glory be!" she chuckled. "Nothing is weird to gleamers."

I guess I had forgotten who I was talking to. Luke, the kidnapper...He may have thought he was being paid for child laborers, but I think the farms are actually camps run by the Murk."

Nana sighed but didn't respond. As usual, she wasn't surprised by anything I said.

"You know what the Murk are, don't you? Why didn't you tell me?"

"What are the camps for?" she asked.

"I-I don't know."

"Yes, you do. Concentrate. What are they for?"

I did know what I thought. I just didn't want to say it. "Brainwashing. To...To destroy their hope and..."

"And what?"

"I don't know."

"Build an army," she replied.

"Nana, why do you know about this?"

"The Murk are centuries old. They've always been. They have a spiritual army, but if they can build an army in the physical realm, they are more likely to destroy what they hate."

"Which is what?"

"Charity."

Charity? Is that a person?

"If they can fill those kids with darkness and replace hope with despair—"

"You mean program them?"

"Yes."

"But I stopped it, right?"

"The ones that are taken are always returned home to eventually spread hate. The younger they can start on them, the better."

"Why didn't you tell me about the Murk?"

"There's a time for everything." Nana reached over and held my hand.

"It's not over, is it?"

"For now. But the Murk is always at work." She looked into my eyes. "Your gleam is even brighter now. I think I know your destiny."

"Really?" My voice perked up and then came back down. "You're not going to tell me, are you?"

"You'll know in time, sugar." Nana stood. "Let's get some nourishment in you before you pass out for another day."

<hr />

I know my mom was happy she didn't have to drive me to school anymore since the kidnapper had been caught. And I was glad because she always ran late. Plus, I enjoyed my walks. The morning was peaceful and gave me time to think as I kicked at the fallen leaves along the sidewalk.

I thought about Dingy's rescue, what Nana said about the Murk, and about Principal Vernon. I had a feeling he would call me into his office sometime that day. *That should be interesting*, I thought.

But, the main thing on my mind was my guardian angel. Dingy's rescue was as good a time as any for him to appear. I thought it was Ariel, but she didn't appear. Principal

Vernon did, but it couldn't be him. Could it? And my friends were there, but that wasn't anything out of the ordinary. I saw no signs of a divine being, so what was up? I was in battle. Why didn't he show himself?

———✁———

Just like I thought, I was called down to the principal's office. I sat in front of Principal Vernon watching him pace behind his desk.

"Understand that I really don't want to do this, but rules are rules."

"I understand."

"I mean I believe—I don't know what I believe…. But you still have detention because of the fight with Cameron."

"I'll be there."

He sat down. "I don't understand any of this…" The phone on his desk buzzed, but he ignored it.

"My wife has cancer. You knew that?"

"I only knew she's sick."

"Because you saw it?"

"Yes."

"And that's what happened with the little boy?"

"Yes."

He shook his head, as if he were trying to understand. "Okay," he said as he placed his palms flat on the desk while looking down at them. He lifted his head. "No more acts of heroism. You could've been killed. I know your parents have probably already given you the same speech, but they weren't there. I *saw* what happened. You have to think about your safety. Really, Sheena. If there is a problem, come to me."

"Yes, sir."

I stood, even though he didn't say the conversation was over.

Principal Vernon looked up at me but didn't stand. There was a question on his face behind weary eyes. A door opened without me even touching him this time.

"She will live," I replied to the question that wasn't asked.

Principal Vernon slumped back into his chair, as if a huge weight had been lifted from his body.

I turned and left his office, walking as fast as I could down the hall. I stopped around the corner and leaned my head back against the wall. I don't know why I felt so much anxiety over what had just happened. It was unreal that I had just told him that, or even saw what I saw, again.

The ever-changing life of a gleamer. That's what I had to get used to. This was my life now.

At lunch, Teddy sat on the edge of the table as if there weren't open seats all around us. "Look Sheena, I know you've had a lot going on with gleameration business and all—"

"Gleameration is not a word, Teddy," I said as I bit into my turkey wrap.

He stared at my hands. "That looks good. Let me have a bite."

"No, I don't do other people's saliva on my food. Here." I tossed him the other wrap from my bag. "Finish what you were saying."

He peeled back the parchment paper from the wrap and took a bite. "Because of everything that's been going on I haven't brought this up, but Comic-Con is coming back to Grand Rapids, and we need to be there."

"We would have to find someone to drive us all the way to Grand Rapids. Not only that, we're all grounded."

"That's only like forty minutes away. And we're grounded with benefits because we did a good thing."

"You might be right about that. Might."

"Who are we going to be this time?"

"Why can't we just wear superhero t-shirts instead of costumes?"

"Well, you were Sailor Moon last time."

"That was so three-years-ago. I wouldn't dare."

"Girls have so many options now."

"What are you guys talking about?" asked Chana as she sat with her tray.

I looked over everything she'd purchased for lunch, checking if I wanted to take anything. *Maybe the pudding.*

"Comic-Con."

"It's coming back?"

"Yep."

"Ooo, that's tough. I'm grounded for life."

"Give them time to calm down."

Chana shook her head. "My dad wants me to pee in a cup every week now. Drugs, really? I would never."

"He's just angry about his truck. He knows better than that."

"I don't know—"

"Look. Why is he sitting over there, staring?" asked Teddy with his mouth stuffed.

"Maybe he wants to join us," Chana replied.

"I don't know, but we're all cool now, right? I mean, he really came through for me."

"I'll be back," said Teddy, eyeing Cameron as he walked away.

I guess we were all skeptical about if we were really friends now or what. Bradly wasn't exactly being buddy-buddy, but she waved at me that morning while the other FPS looked at her with an expression that asked, *Why is she talking to her?*

I nudged Chana, seeing Cameron stand and approach us.

"Sheena, can I talk to you?" he asked.

Chana stepped in front of me. "No."

I tried to move her out of the way. "What's wrong with you?"

"Nothing. He can say whatever he wants to say right here in front of me."

Oh my gosh, I thought. She really didn't want any boy talking to me except Teddy.

"Chana..."

"Fine, but don't think I didn't see you act like you didn't see us this morning when you were with your friends," Chana said, looking back as she walked away.

"What's up her butt?" Cameron yelled toward Chana, "Yo, Crazy, chill. Did it cross your mind that I really *didn't* see you? We're cool now, remember? Don't make me pop you." He turned to me. "Sheesh, why is she acting stupid? I mean, I'm talking to you right now in front of my friends and the whole lunchroom. Did she consider that?"

"Hey, remember the other Cameron that was in my shed, can I speak with him? Can you bring him into the light?"

"Ha! You're trying to say I have multiple personalities. That's funny. But, uh...I just realized that I never apologized to you about Theodore's journal."

"We're past that. You helped save my life, remember?"

"Yeah, well I, uh, I..."

"What? Just say it."

"Do you have a date for the dance?"

If you are shocked inside, does it always show on your face? I hoped it didn't. "No..."

Cameron smiled.

"I don't think I'm going."

His expression didn't just drop, his whole body slumped. "Okay...Well...I was asking for, uh, someone."

"Okay. Why don't you, I mean have that someone, ask Ariel?"

"The weird girl?"

"She's not weird."

"Yes, she is, and not only that, I don't think she can afford a dress."

"Why would you say that?"

He looked as if he wasn't sure he should tell me. Again, I was shocked. Cameron usually told whatever he knew.

"I think they live in their car," he whispered.

"Don't lie like that. You don't say things like that about people. You're a Pastor's son. You should know better." I was offended for Ariel.

"Calm down."

Chana ran over. "What? What did he say?"

"He thinks Ariel is homeless."

"I can see that. Are you sure?" Chana asked with less attitude than when she'd left.

"What did you see?" I asked.

"She arrived at school early one day and washed up at school."

"How do you know she washed up?"

"She changed clothes. I assumed she washed up."

"That's not enough to go on."

He looked down at the floor. "Well, I was at the store with my dad late at night and saw them in their car."

"That doesn't mean anything."

"How many people do you know that sit at the back of the parking lot in the car and never start it up?" He dug into his pocket. "And then there's this..."

"Where did you find that?"

13

I snatched the star bracelet from Cameron's hand. Ariel didn't go anywhere without that bracelet. I remembered how she reacted when I gave it to her after it had broken off her wrist. She looked panicked.

"I'll see you guys later. I need to find her."

"Sheena," Chana called. "This isn't for you to fix."

"Oww!" Cameron exclaimed behind me. "Stop punching people."

"You run your mouth too much," said Chana.

I really didn't know where to find Ariel. I didn't even know what I was going to say to her when I did. She hadn't come to the lunchroom, so I checked in the library, and walked up and down each aisle of books, looking for her. From the library window, I could see Principal Vernon walking down the hall.

I ran out of the library. "Mr. Vernon," I yelled.

He turned toward me as I ran. "I have a question..."

He waited. I knew what I wanted to say, but I couldn't figure out how to start.

"What's wrong, Sheena?"

"If you find out someone is homeless, can you help them?"

"One of our students? Do you know that one of our students is homeless?"

"No. I mean I'm not sure yet. But if they are, can you help?"

Please say yes. Please say yes.

He looked out ahead of him, in thought. "There are agencies that can help—"

I shook my head. My voice rose. "No, they would need to be helped immediately."

"Sheena, calm down. I will see that they are helped. Okay?"

"Okay..." I backed away.

Principal Vernon watched me. I know he thought that I saw something with a student, but I didn't. I didn't see anything about Ariel. I think that's what was getting me so worked up. What good was being a gleamer if I couldn't help those I cared about?

I never found Ariel, and she didn't come to class after lunch. In fact, while home from school, I realized how many days of school she actually missed. She always wore the same things to school—jeans, t-shirt, and a hoodie tied around her waist—like she only owned a couple of outfits. She never brought lunch, never wore a backpack, and I never saw or met her parents. And she was always at the school early, as Cameron had said. I had thought all of this was because she was really my angel.

Had I missed all the signs that something was wrong? How could I call myself a true friend, being so caught up in my own world that I didn't recognize what was going on with Ariel?

Selfish, just selfish, I thought, mentally beating myself up.

That night at dinner, my mom's eyes were on me every time I glanced up, like there was something she wanted to tell me, or ask.

"Your dad drove for the first time since the accident," she said with a laugh.

I slowly forked over my fried cabbage and tried to act interested.

"I was terrified, but he did just fine."

"I guess he won't have to work from home anymore."
My mom didn't respond. Finally, she asked, "Did you have any gleams today?"

"Mom!"

"Your dad's asleep. Did you?"

"No, mom. It doesn't work like that. I don't walk around having gleams all day. And I can't see what's happening with every single person," I said, dropping my fork.

"Why are you so agitated? What happened?"

"Nothing."

"Yes, something did. No more secrets, remember?"

"One of my friends didn't come to school. I'm worried about her—the girl that almost got kidnapped."

"Oh." My mom put her fork down. "Did you try calling her?"

"I thought you said I can't use my phone unless it's an emergency because I'm grounded?"

"Again, did you try calling her?"

She knew I was using it anyway. "Her phone is off."

My mom leaned back against her chair while staring at her plate. "I don't really know what to say, Sheena. I know how you get. Things like this become a project for you, and you start your investigations, taking it on as if your life depends on it."

She really did know me.

"Do you know where she lives?"

"I have an idea."

My mom sighed. "Well, get your jacket. Let's go."

I think I leaped over the table. I don't know. I jumped into my mom's arms and held her like I was four years old.

We drove to the supermarket that Cameron mentioned.

"Did you need something from here?" my mom asked.

"No… She lives near here."

"Near the parking lot? But there are no—" My mom stopped the car in the middle of the lane. "Sheena, are they homeless?"

"I heard they might be."

I noticed a man walking a little boy to a van at the back of the lot. "Mom, pull back there where that man is.

"Excuse me, Sir." I called out the window.

He turned toward me, and I couldn't believe how much he looked like Ariel. "Are you Ariel's dad? Mr. Knight? She wasn't at school and—"

"Ariel's gone," the little boy that was with him said.

The man looked exhausted, but not from working too hard or working out. Maybe from life in general.

"Yes, I'm Ariel's father." He walked toward our car. "Today is the anniversary of her mom's passing. It's always hard on her. We've been looking for her. Do *you* have any idea where she could be?"

"I don't, but we can search, right, Mom?"

"Yes, we can," she replied.

"I would think she's somewhere where she'd feel safe this late in the evening. She wasn't at the church she's been visiting."

Safe?

"Mom, I know where she is," I whispered.

We drove to the school and got out of the car. My mom walked me to the back of the property.

"Someone's over there."

"That's her."

"How did you know she would be here?"

"Because there's this game we play at lunch, and that table is base. When I explained the game, I told her, 'Base means we're safe here. Nothing can touch us.' It was the strange way she looked at me when I said it."

"I'll wait here," my mom said.

I walked over to the dark figure sitting at the picnic table.

"You shouldn't be out here alone at night."

"Sheena..."

I didn't scare her, and she didn't sound surprised. I'd never seen her so down, like she didn't care about anything.

"What are you doing here?"

"I was worried about you, and so is your dad."

"You talked to my dad?"

"Yes."

I sat next to her. The best thing I could do was be there for her, not try to act like I knew what she was going through. I couldn't possibly understand. My mom was right here with me, and we had a home and food.

We sat in silence for a while.

"So, you know my secret?"

"Everyone has secrets."

It was a few minutes before she spoke again. "I don't want to be taken away from my dad."

"I wouldn't worry about that. I think you guys are going to be okay."

She looked at me. "Really?"

"Yes."

Her voice cracked. "I really, really, miss my mom...But I'm not mad at God anymore. I just miss her."

I didn't know what to say.

"And I lost the bracelet she made for me. It was the only thing I had left from her." She held her arm up. "I even have a suntan from where the lines of the star were."
I looked, but it was too dark for me to see anything. "She called me her little angel from beyond the stars."

I held out my hand to her. "Ariel, look."

Ariel gasped. "Sheena!"

I imagined the huge grin on her face because I couldn't see her well.

"Where did you find it?"

"I upgraded it for you. Every now and then I get back into making jewelry with my mom. I added leather straps and a clasp to help it stay—"

Oof! The wind was knocked out of me when Ariel hugged and squeezed me.

"Okay, okay," I laughed. "Can we go now? Maybe you need to see it in the light before you make up your mind that you like it."

Ariel stood, and we walked over to my mom, who always knows just the right thing to say. Hopefully, I would develop that skill one day.

"I hear we have a new member of the family," she said, hugging Ariel.

My parents and our church paid for Ariel's family to stay in a hotel until the agency Principal Vernon talked about found them a home.

I wouldn't have believed Ariel could've become any happier a kid than she already was. I kept thinking, *I had something to do with her happiness. I helped someone. I could get used to this.*

Did all of this prove Ariel wasn't my guardian angel? Not necessarily. However, I did kind of feel like I was hers. If she was my guardian angel, I decided I would wait patiently for her to reveal it. And I knew it was going to be something grand—maybe an angel surrounded by heavenly light and sparkles. That would be cool.

14

Ariel didn't miss school anymore and hung out with me and Chana all the time now. And Chana was even nice to her. We walked together to gym class after lunch period.

"Are you going to the dance, Ariel?"

"No, I don't think so."

"Isn't there someone you would like to ask?"

"Nope."

"We can go together if you want to go. Lots of kids attend without a date." I was grounded, but I knew I could talk my parents into easing up for one night so I could accompany Ariel.

"Sheena, I'm sure there are many boys that would like to go with you."

"No, I don't think so. Maybe If I looked like her." I pointed at one of the FPS with the ends of her hair dyed blue.

"I like her hair."

"Yeah, everyone does."

Ariel grabbed my hands. "You're just as pretty as she is. Just wait, someone is going to ask you."

I laughed to myself. *She always grabs my hands like she's my mom.* But from the moment she touched them, I felt a happy kind of peace come over me. It was weird. I guess her happy was infectious. She released my hands and pushed the door open for the girls' locker room.

We each grabbed a red bathing suit from the shelf and headed to the lockers to put our things away. Then we changed, entered the showers, and rinsed off before going through the pool door.

The air was warm and moist from the heated pool and smelled of chlorine. There were a lot of us in that class. All girls. All wearing the same red bathing suit and white swim cap. A third of us couldn't swim and that included me. I could float like nobody's business, but I didn't know how to tread water.

I enjoyed the class though. Chana was there also, but she could swim, so she was on the deep end most of the time with the swimmers.

My group practiced the breaststroke in the shallow end of the pool. Somehow, I switched to the doggy paddle. I just thought it was funny.

For the last portion of class, we were to swim along the entire pool along the wall. Ariel and I got separated because I moved ahead. The girls were moving too slow, so

I cut across on the diagonal. I think Ariel tried to follow me, but I didn't know until I was almost to the rope at the middle point of the pool. Chana was swimming past the shallow end.

I held onto the wall with one hand while wiping my eyes with the other and turned, looking behind me.

Ariel was too far from the wall. She dipped below the water.

What is she doing?

The girls were still moving along the wall and going around me. Ariel bobbed up and back under again.

Oh my gosh, is she drowning?

I didn't know what to do, and no one was paying attention. So, I did the only thing I *could* do. I put my feet against the wall and pushed out to propel my body toward her.

My eyes were closed. I hadn't gotten to the point where I'd open them underwater yet. It was hard enough adjusting to water in my ears. I was now Aquaman soaring through a chlorinated sea. At least that's what I imagined.

I felt a bump as I hit Ariel. I grabbed ahold of her, only I didn't know how to get her to the wall. I laid back, swallowed water, and began choking.

I pushed her forward as I went under and tried to kick my legs and move my arms as I'd seen Chana do when she treads water, but it wasn't working. I moved my legs faster, like I was riding a bike.

I heard muffled laughing. *They think I'm joking around?* My head bobbed up and then I sunk below again. I knew that was the last time I was going up, as my arms and legs thrashed about.

I held my breath until I couldn't anymore....

15

"It's so dark. Where am I?"

"In the hospital."

"Who are you? Are you my angel?"

"I am Javan, I am Mr. Tobias, I am Nana, I am..."

"You've been with me all the time?"

"I've traveled through people to get to know you. I saw you through their eyes."

"Why?"

"Because you asked."

The dark area began to brighten. I saw flowers of every color and every kind, roses and tulips, hydrangeas, and flowers I'd never seen before. But they shined brightly, as if they were plugged in. I'd never seen anything like it. I looked around at my neighborhood—except it wasn't my neighborhood. Everything was just better and there was a feeling of peace and love and joy. The sparkling flowers made the area look magical. But I couldn't see me. I felt weightless.

"Is this heaven?"

"No."

"Why have you stayed around?"

"You wanted to talk to me. You wanted to thank me."

"You're leaving now?"

"I must. And you must also. You have so much hope in your heart for the world. Do not let that hope die. It is how you will defeat the Murk."

"I have to defeat the Murk? I can do that?"

"Have faith, Little Gleamer."

I felt him pulling away. "Wait, please don't leave. Are you my guardian angel? You're Ariel, right? All the signs have been there. I knew that was you. You kept doing things. Smelling like flowers and appearing places, and always watching me and sticking with me. Oh, and you fixed my nail."

"I was not Ariel."

"You, weren't? You're saying she's just a regular kid?"

"Thank you for saving her. She is a version of mankind that shines brighter than most. For this reason, she must live. She too, has a special gift."

I was confused. She wasn't a normal kid. She had to be an angel. "But she—"

"I was not her."

"Will I ever see you again?"

"If it is allowed. It is not necessary now. There is much for you to learn. You have a special gift, and even with that gift, you never noticed your true guardian angel. She's been with you since you were a child."

"She? As in Nana? I knew it!"

"No, not Nana."

"My mom?

"No, look deeper. Sometimes your best friend is actually a guardian angel in disguise. Your guardian will help prepare you for what is to come."

A bright light began to expand, engulfing everything.

"Wait!" I tried to run after him, but I couldn't feel that I was going anywhere, like I didn't have feet and legs or a body at all. "Don't leave!"

All of a sudden, I was aware of everything around me. The people and paramedics, the burning in my lungs. I was alive and looked up, seeing light dissipate over my head.

I had never stayed overnight in a hospital as a patient before. Now I knew how my dad felt. Well, not really, I wasn't in the type of accident he'd been in, nor did I have the same kind of injuries. They were just keeping me under observation. There wasn't much on television, but my mom brought my laptop, so that helped with my boredom.

"You have a visitor, young lady," said the nurse while leaving the room.

Chana walked in. "She-She, I was so worried about you." Her eyes were red, like she'd been crying. She smiled at me. "Are you okay? My mom said I can stay as long as I want. I can even spend the night. Do you think they'll roll another bed in here? I can sleep in that chair. Does it recline? Or you can just scooch over. Why are you looking at me like that?"

I smiled at her. "You're such a cry baby."

"You better not ever, ever-ever-ever, scare me like that again."

I angled my head at her and looked into her eyes. There it was, that twinkle.

"I'm sorry I couldn't see you for who you were."

"What are you talking about? You know who I am. I'm your best friend. And you better not bring up Theodore. He's second."

"You're more than that. You're the reason I shot through the pool and saved Ariel. I can't even swim. I couldn't do that."

"But you almost drowned."

"Really? Almost? Where were you? On the other side of the pool, right? I should have drowned, but it was you who pulled me out, wasn't it?"

"I think you hit your head on the wall of the pool or something." She placed my hand over the bandage.

"Ouch! It's tender."

"See, you banged it. Look at your nails, all chipped up. I'm going to go and get some polish. What color do you want?"

"Pink."

"I think they have some in the gift shop, and I need to do something about that hair before Theodore comes up here. I'll be back, and when you get out of here, we'll start the search for your angel again."

"No need."

Her eyes perked up. "Why not? Has there been a new development?"

"My guardian angel is always with me."

Chana smiled, and as she turned, the same bright light that surrounded the archangel surrounded her. She winked at me and held a finger to her lips.

The end
Well, not really...

As I walked through the front door of my house, a dark-haired man wearing a camel coat was leaving.

"Dad, who was that?"

"Mr. Tobias's son. Mr. Tobias had added you to his will. Did you know that? He left this for you."

My mom and I glanced at each other as my dad handed me something large wrapped in brown paper.

I took the package back to the kitchen table and tore off the wrapping. It was an old leather-bound book about two inches thick and the size of a big photo album book. You know, the kind your grandparents always have. There was a brass symbol on the cover, loops that connected at the center of a circle, and there were symbols carved along an outer circle.

My mom stood so close to me, anxious to see inside.

I opened the book and slammed it shut, shocked by what I'd seen.

"What is it?" she asked. "You couldn't have read anything that fast."

"His son said they looked at it but weren't able to read it," my dad replied, while heading for the back door.

The scent of barbequed meat drifted in as the door opened. Knowing my dad, he was trying to surprise me with my favorite turkey burgers that only he knew how to make.

I grabbed the book from the table and held it to my chest.

"What is it, Sheena?" my mom half-whispered.

"I-I don't know yet. I don't know if I'm ready to think about Mr. Tobias being gone."

She exhaled as if she'd been holding her breath and rubbed my shoulders. "I can understand that. How about we light up the fire pit and sit out in the fresh air before it gets too cold?"

I nodded, looking down at the floor. I couldn't make eye contact. Not yet. She would know I lied. How could I tell her I just saw my willow in that book?

"What would you like, warm apple cider or lemon tea?"

I wanted the apple cider, because with it usually came mini powder sugared donuts, but I chose the tea, because my throat didn't quite feel back to normal yet after my almost drowning.

My mom sat in a chair in front of the steel fire pit, sipping tea. I sat on a blanket under my willow tree, leaned back against it, and smiled while watching my dad flip burgers and joke with my mom that he would burn hers until it was like charcoal if she kept nagging him.

Flames danced over the wood of the pit, and just above it the air wavered from the heat, blurring the look of the chair on the other side of the pit. It made me think of the Murk. They wavered like that in the wind. I set my cup down and picked up the book that lay on the ground beside me, carefully placing it on my lap. My finger traced over the swirls of the symbol on the cover.

"Sheena, what's on your mind?" asked my dad, glancing over.

I shook my head. "Just thinking about how mysterious the world is."

My eyes met my mom's eyes. Hers had been wide, as if on alert.

"We think we know everything about everything, but we don't," I continued.

"Hmm...that's true."

My mom's eyes softened. I don't think she was sure of what I might say. She relaxed and showed a hint of a smile.

"Jonas, watch what you're doing!" she exclaimed. She threw her blanket to the side, grabbed a jug from the table, and ran over to my dad.

Good. Their focus was off me, and on the flames of the grill.

I gently lifted the cover of the leather-bound book. It was so old, I thought it might creak like our stairs, or possibly fall apart. My eyes widened as I turned the pages. I sat forward. The entire book was written in the same symbols that I'd seen in my dream—known only to angels, unreadable by humans.

But I understood them...

BUT THERE'S MORE...

Thank you for reading
The Girl Who Spoke to the Wind.
Would you like a special prologue featuring what
happened to Mr. Tobias and more information on
Sheena's mystery, exclusive to my VIP List?
Then join today at: https://www.lbanne.com/vip-club

Please Leave A Review

Your review means the world to me. I greatly appreciate any kind words. Even one or two sentences go a long way. The number of reviews a book receives greatly improves how well it does on Amazon. Even a short review would be wonderful. Thank you in advance.

Review here: https://www.amazon.com/dp/B08179VLXY

ABOUT THE AUTHOR

L. B. Anne is best known for her Lolo and Winkle book series, in which tells humorous stories of middle-school siblings, Lolo and Winkle, based on her youth, growing up in Queens, New York. She lives on the Gulf Coast of Florida with her husband and is a full-time author and speaker. When she's not inventing new obstacles for her diverse characters to overcome, you can find her reading, playing bass guitar, running on the beach, or downing a mocha iced coffee at a local cafe while dreaming of being your favorite author.

Visit L. B. at www.lbanne.com

Facebook: facebook.com/authorlbanne

Instagram: Instagram.com/authorlbanne

Twitter: twitter.com/authorlbanne

Made in the USA
Las Vegas, NV
29 December 2020